Without Restraint

BECAUSE NAUGHTY CAN BE OH SO NICE®

NE LTD

By Nicole Edwards

The Alluring Indulgence Series
Kaleb
Zane
Travis
Holidays with the Walker Brothers
Ethan
Braydon
Sawyer
Brendon

The Austin Arrows Series
Rush
Kaufman

The Bad Boys of Sports Series
Bad Reputation
Bad Business

The Caine Cousins Series
Hard to Hold
Hard to Handle

The Club Destiny Series
Conviction
Temptation
Addicted
Seduction
Infatuation
Captivated
Devotion
Perception
Entrusted
Adored
Distraction

The Coyote Ridge Series
Curtis
Jared

The Dead Heat Ranch Series
Boots Optional
Betting on Grace
Overnight Love
By Nicole Edwards (cont.)

Without Restraint

Devil's Playground
Book 2

NICOLE EDWARDS

Nicole Edwards Limited
PO Box 806
Hutto, Texas 78634
www.slipublishing.com
www.NicoleEdwardsLimited.com

Without Restraint – A Devil's Playground novella is a work of fiction. Names, characters, businesses, places, events and incidents either are the products of the author's imagination or used in a fictitious manner. Any resemblance to actual persons, living or dead, business establishments, events, or locales is entirely coincidental.

Cover Image: © essl | 123rf.com (38721374)
Cover Design: © Nicole Edwards Limited
Editing: Blue Otter Editing www.BlueOtterEditing.com

ISBN (ebook): 978-1-939786-74-6
ISBN (print): 978-1-939786-73-9

1

Tuesday night

"Don't move," Micah Fontenot groaned softly.

The body beneath his was warm, solid. Almost enough but not quite...

"Deeper, Micah," Hayden growled roughly, his fingers linking with Micah's as Micah held on to him, grounding him in the moment.

Micah wasn't sure he could go much deeper. He was lodged to the hilt in Hayden's phenomenal body, the same way he'd been for the past three fucking months. And though the sex was fucking fantastic, it was never enough.

Micah rolled his hips forward, pressing his lips against the back of Hayden's neck, enjoying the sultry, spicy scent of the man.

"Yes," Hayden hissed. "More."

Micah rested his forehead on Hayden's shoulder as he lifted his hips and pushed forward again, Hayden's ass gripping his dick.

"Need more," Micah mumbled, hating that he did.

What he and Hayden had … it was sensational. For the most part, it was completely physical, and the sex was off the charts. Day, night. Didn't matter when or where, they could fuck like teenagers and Micah would never get enough of the man, but at the same time, he never got enough of... Of *what*, he had no fucking clue. He needed something more. Something more than Hayden could give him.

And Micah fucking hated himself for that. Hated that he was different, that he couldn't be content with the good thing he had going.

Suddenly, the solid body beneath his was shifting. Micah's dick dislodged from Hayden's ass, and the next thing he knew, he was flat on his stomach with Hayden's weight on top of him, pushing him into the mattress.

"Don't move," Hayden warned, nipping Micah's ear, the weight of him straddling Micah's thighs. "Gonna make this good for you."

Micah took deep breaths, lying there in the darkened hotel room, waiting for whatever the fuck Hayden would do to him. It was always like this. They started out hot and heavy, but halfway through, Micah's brain kicked in, ruining the moment and screwing shit up for them both.

Hayden's warmth disappeared momentarily, then returned in all its exquisite glory. Only this time, Micah could tell Hayden had sheathed himself with a condom and was beginning to prepare Micah's ass with his fingers.

"Oh, yes," Micah moaned, pushing his hips back against the intrusion.

Hayden teased for long seconds, but then his cock breached Micah's ass, pushing in slowly, stretching him perfectly.

"This what you need?" Hayden whispered in the dark. "You need my dick in your ass?"

Micah nodded. He needed that and more, but Hayden already knew that.

"Or how about my dick in your ass while your dick's lodged in a sweet, wet pussy? Is that what you want?"

Aww, fuck. The visual that created made Micah's dick jump to attention. The thought of fucking a sweet, willing woman while Hayden fucked him... It was his fantasy. The only thing he could think about these days. He knew he was warped and twisted because he couldn't find what he needed in only one person, but he couldn't deny it. He was bisexual. He craved a man *and* a woman. Only he wanted them at the same fucking time.

"God, yes," Hayden groaned, pumping his hips, filling Micah's ass. "I want a woman between us," he continued. "I want to watch while she rides your dick and I fuck your mouth, Micah."

Micah's dick twitched, blood rushing faster through his veins.

"And I want to fuck her at the same time you do. Both of us ... lodged deep inside her... Can you imagine that, Micah?"

Fuck yes, he could. He could and he did. All the fucking time.

Hayden began fucking Micah deeper, making him moan as he imagined what it would be like for a woman to be right there with them. He'd slept with his fair share of both men and women in his lifetime, but never had he had the pleasure of two at once. Considering he lived in Sin City, it would've been so easy for him to do, but he'd held off, scared he'd get addicted to it, that he would never be satisfied one on one again. And maybe that was the problem. Maybe he'd thought about it too much already.

"That's it, baby," Hayden rumbled against his ear. "Think about your mouth on that sweet pussy while I drill your ass with my dick. You want that?"

"Yes…" Micah pressed his hips back, forcing Hayden deeper. "Oh, fuck, yes."

"Or how about she eats your ass while I suck your dick? Both of us driving you wild with our mouths. That what you want?"

"Oh, God." Micah's body hummed. He wasn't going to last much longer.

But he got the feeling that had been Hayden's plan all along.

2

Hayden Wellington did his absolute best not to come too soon, but it wasn't easy. The way Micah's ass clasped his dick … the sensations were so fucking good it hurt.

But he held back because he knew all too well what Micah was going through, even if Micah didn't quite understand it himself. It was one of the things that had attracted Hayden to the man from the beginning. Ever since Micah and his twin brother, Isaiah, started managing Devil's Playground a few years ago, Hayden had been attracted to him. Fiercely.

Initially, he'd managed to keep his distance because they worked together. Being that they both handled security for Devil's Playground and for the big boss when he came into town, Hayden hadn't wanted to make things weird.

Turned out that attraction was mutual, so keeping his hands to himself hadn't been necessary.

"Fuck me, Hayden. Now!" Micah bellowed.

Hayden gripped Micah's hips and pulled him up onto his knees, allowing for better leverage. With one hand cupping Micah's shoulder, Hayden began fucking him. Hard. Slamming home, retreating, slamming in again. Over and over he fucked them both into oblivion, never stopping. He tried to mutter the things he knew Micah wanted to hear … all the fantasies Hayden had already played out in his head a million times. It usually worked for Micah, but he knew one day, the fantasies wouldn't be enough. For either of them.

At some point, they would have to find something more, something real that could sate all of their urges. Hayden wouldn't deny that being with Micah was phenomenal, but it wasn't enough. So damn close, just not quite…

"Stroke your dick," Hayden commanded. "Imagine a woman's hot fucking mouth wrapped around it, sucking hard while I pound your ass."

"Oh, fuck … Hay… Oh, shit…"

"That's it, baby. I want you to come for me."

Hayden doubled his efforts, chasing his own release while Micah continued fighting for his own.

"One of these days…" Hayden slammed his hips hard against Micah's ass. "We're gonna find that woman who can handle both of us. And when we do … it'll be just the three of us."

"Fuck!" Micah cried out, his body jerking as he came, triggering Hayden's release.

Stilling his hips, he leaned over Micah as his dick pulsed, filling the condom. They both collapsed onto the bed in a heap of sweaty limbs, but Hayden didn't pull away. He rolled to the side, keeping one arm over Micah as they caught their breath.

It'd been three months since they'd started this exclusive fucking thing. It wasn't as though they'd planned it; things had merely worked out that way, and it worked for them. Considering how long they'd known each other, and the few random one-nighters they'd had over the years, it only made sense. Not to mention, Hayden had developed feelings for Micah long ago. He wasn't sure the same could be said in reverse, yet he held out hope.

Micah wasn't the type to talk about his feelings. Fantasies, sure. Desires, yes. But emotions were off-limits. Instead, they focused on fetishes and needs, both of them admitting that they wanted and needed the same thing. It worked for them.

But in the last few weeks, he'd noticed Micah's growing agitation. He'd always been dark and brooding, but ever since Micah's twin brother, Isaiah, had fallen in love, Micah had been pulling away. Not necessarily from Hayden, more so from everyone in general. Those sexy smiles that had once been a prominent fixture on Micah's face had all but disappeared. It was as though Micah was always lost in his own head. Always.

And Hayden knew why.

Unfortunately, he also knew that until they found that woman who could handle being with both of them ... at the same time ... this would be all they had.

And, like Micah, Hayden had already started wanting more.

3

Saturday night

Lindy Weatherford walked into the VIP section of Devil's Playground a little after ten on Saturday night. Due to Vegas's lenient smoking laws, there was a thin haze of smoke throughout, while red lights glowed from the corners. The music was sexy, a deep, throbbing bass that Lindy could feel vibrating in her belly. The overall vibe was sensual, mysterious. This area was vastly different from the club downstairs, which had strobe lights galore and sweaty, writhing bodies crammed together throughout.

Nope, up here, the bodies weren't touching out of necessity, they were touching because they wanted to. And oh, boy, were they touching.

Without Restraint

Trying not to stare, Lindy glanced around the room. The ambience was intriguing. The thump of the music reverberated off the walls, but it remained low enough that people could talk without yelling. Her eyes moved toward the bar, where she noticed waitresses getting drinks to deliver to the various guests.

Squinting, Lindy took stock of the people closest to her. She was supposed to be meeting friends, but based on their apparent absence, they'd long ago ditched her for whatever or whomever. Had her friends not insisted on coming here, Lindy knew she would've never ventured into this scene. Heck, she almost felt out of place.

It wasn't the first time she'd been stood up by her friends, Lindy thought. At twenty-nine, she had spent more than one evening alone at her cramped apartment, doing nothing more than vegging on the couch and watching Netflix. In fact, it was her preferred evening activity after spending the day crunching numbers.

Well, before *The Talk*, that was.

Her best friend, Tabitha, had kindly informed her that Lindy was quickly getting older and she'd become that humdrum friend other friends didn't want to call to go out. Unfortunately, Lindy hadn't been able to come up with anything in her defense because ... well, because she *had* become that friend.

It had been a wake-up call, sure.

Maneuvering through the groups of people lingering on wide, black leather couches, Lindy looked for an empty seat. She probably wouldn't stay long, but she owed it to herself to at least have a drink and wait to see if her friends had in fact ditched her. She seriously doubted she was the first to arrive, but stranger things had happened.

If Lindy was as boring as Tabitha claimed, she wouldn't put it past them to have made their way to one of the other clubs on the strip.

Perhaps they were merely freshening up in the ladies' room. Doubtful but possible.

Lindy wasn't worried about being popular, but she damn sure didn't want to be *that* friend. Always the one to tell it like it is, Tabitha had harped on the subject until Lindy had no choice but to take a good long look at herself in the proverbial mirror.

Seriously, Lindy. The only thing left for you to do is get a cat and some support hose. Then you'll be right at home with the geriatric set.

Yep, Tabitha had a way of saying what was on her mind.

Turned out, Tabitha was right.

So, when Lindy had taken an introspective look at herself, what she found looking back at her was a woman who had absolutely zero stories to tell. While her friends went on and on about this adventure or that, Lindy was always the one listening in. She didn't even have a one-night-stand story to share. The only sex she'd ever had had taken place in a semi-committed relationship, at least. And even those had been few and far between.

Seriously, how hard could a one-night stand be? A little talking, some making out, a nice roll in the sheets. That was doable. Then, Lindy could get back to her humdrum life, but at least she'd have a story to tell over wine with the girls.

Oddly enough, that was the one thing she'd focused on since her conversation with Tabitha. She wanted to have a one-night stand. She wanted to let loose at least once. She wanted to do the dreaded walk of shame in the morning, then go back to the real world and surround herself with the wealth of boring she'd accumulated over the years.

Lindy stopped walking, peering around again. She glanced in the farthest corner, but there weren't any empty spots. Every inch of seating was occupied by…

Wait.

The red lights from above shined down on the various occupants, most of which were…

Oh, my God. They weren't simply touching; they were… Was that girl topless? And was she…?

What the fuck was this place?

It wasn't a strip club; she knew that much. Which meant these people were doing these things willingly to one another. In public. Holy moly.

A warm body pressed up against her back and Lindy's spine stiffened.

"Looking for someone?"

The deep, rich baritone rumbled in her ear, drowning out the sultry bass beat echoing off the walls.

"I think I'm in the wrong place," she replied, pivoting slowly and taking a small step back to put some space between herself and the man who owned the deep voice.

Holy shit.

Piercing brown eyes set in a face that could only be described as beautiful stared back at her. His dark brown hair was a little long on top, reflecting the red glow that filled the space. His thick eyebrows arched up as his mesmerizing eyes slowly perused her face.

Lindy suddenly felt underdressed in the skimpy black dress and four-inch heels, although she clearly had on more than some of these women here.

"I was..." She fought the urge to look around her. She was fairly certain some of these strangers were having sex while she stood only a few feet away. "I was supposed to meet some friends."

"Supposed to?" he rumbled.

Lindy nodded. "Looks like they've already left."

The guy didn't say anything, but his eyes continued to linger on her face. He never looked down, his gaze never drifting farther than her lips anyway. It was a little off-putting but nice at the same time. Most guys would've been focused on her breasts at this point. Not this guy. He seemed to be studying her.

Heat bloomed in her belly.

"I should probably go home," she said, ignoring her rioting hormones. This guy looked like perfect one-night-stand material.

"A little early to call it a night," he said, his tone warm and low. "Let me buy you a drink."

Lindy knew she should tell him no thank you and head right back out, climb in a cab, and go home.

But something stopped her.

Maybe it was that nagging feeling. The one that said she was going to be a boring old woman with nothing to tell her children. Hell, at this pace, she might never *have* children.

"I'd like that," she found herself saying.

It was now or never.

4

The instant he'd seen her standing in the middle of the crowded room, Micah hadn't been able to take his eyes off the raven-haired beauty. Between that sexy fucking thing she called a dress and those fuck-me heels, he'd been transfixed as soon as she started across the floor of the VIP room.

A woman hadn't caught his eye quite the way she had in a long, long time.

Micah gestured toward the back wall, then placed his other hand on her back, allowing his fingers to brush the smooth skin not covered by the thin silk. He led her past the bouncer who was standing sentry in front of one of the reserved areas. There were fifteen of those areas within the VIP room, all separated by sheer crimson drapes that somehow gave the illusion of privacy although they didn't hamper the view. One deep, long couch with chaise lounges on each end resided boldly in the center while a glass table sat in front of it.

Realizing he hadn't bothered to introduce himself, Micah turned to her and offered his name.

"Lindy Weatherford," she answered sweetly. "It's nice to meet you, Micah."

Micah instantly got the impression that she didn't do this often. For one, she'd seemed a little off-kilter a few minutes ago, her eyes never straying from his face. He got the sense she was trying to avoid looking at the half-dressed— some fully *un*dressed—people enjoying their time in the exclusive section of Devil's Playground.

Without Restraint

Although the main club was like any other outrageous Vegas nightclub with its various rules and enforcers, this part had very little of that. There were no bouncers set out to stop anyone from enjoying a little naked frolicking. If you could afford the cover to get in, you could pretty much make all your voyeuristic fantasies come true. Though, if he were being honest, most people couldn't afford it, which was why those who could wanted to check it out for themselves.

Micah happened to enjoy this part of the club. And the reason he could afford it was due to the fact that he worked at Devil's Playground. His twin brother ran the place, and Micah was the second-in-charge. It paid well, offered a tremendous amount of entertainment, and above all else, Micah enjoyed the scenery.

Especially tonight's scenery.

He wasn't on duty tonight, which was a relief. He'd taken the night off and asked Hayden to join him. He hadn't seen much of the man since Wednesday morning, when Hayden slipped out of his bed and headed back to his own room within the adjoining hotel. Micah had been hoping for a little fantasy play tonight and…

Well, he hadn't anticipated Lindy Weatherford, that was for sure.

Pulling back the sheer curtains, Micah allowed Lindy to step inside. He followed, as did a waitress who'd been standing nearby.

"What would you like to drink?" he asked, urging Lindy to take a seat on the couch.

"Buttery nipple," she said, the color in her cheeks rising.

Micah informed the waitress, then sat down beside Lindy, keeping a safe distance and not getting too comfortable. The woman was a little timid, and the last thing he wanted to do was to scare her off. He'd been known to do that with relative ease. His twin said it was due to his intimidating stare. Whatever the reason, Micah wasn't willing to risk sending this woman running for the hills.

"So, did your friends say where they were going?" he inquired, attempting to make small talk.

Her smile was slow and a little shy. "No."

"Have they done this before? Disappear before you arrive?"

"A couple of times," she stated. "But I can't actually blame them. I'm not exactly the nightclub type, so they probably figured I would be a no-show."

"Do they visit the VIP section often?"

Lindy shook her head. "No." She smiled sweetly. "No way could we afford this. Somehow, my friend got free passes, which is the only reason I'm here."

"But they're not."

"Not that I've seen." Oddly, she didn't sound too disappointed.

"Well, I'm glad they disappeared," he told her honestly.

Her pale blue eyes lingered on his face for a second, and he waited, curious as to what was on her mind. He could tell she was thinking about something. Perhaps she was going to find a gentle way to let him down? Tell him she was ready to call it a night? It was nice to meet him, but this really wasn't her thing?

"I … uh…" Lindy wrung her hands together in her lap.

Micah turned to look at her more fully, unable to resist brushing her long, silky hair back over her shoulder, revealing more creamy skin and a delicate earlobe.

She was petite, probably a foot shorter than him. He didn't usually like women so small, but this one... He didn't know what it was about her. He wanted to think it was the dress, but he'd never been that superficial before. No, it wasn't necessarily what she was wearing, but more the way she wore the dress with confidence yet lacked that haughty air that many women in this particular area often had.

"Can I tell you something, Micah?"

The waitress chose that moment to interrupt, delivering their drinks before disappearing just as quickly.

"Three drinks?" Lindy asked, frowning when she looked back at him.

Rather than explain, he redirected the conversation to her first question. "What did you want to tell me?"

"I've never done this before."

Micah smiled. "*This*?"

"Yeah, you know." She gestured between them. "The one-night-stand thing."

He couldn't help the full-fledged grin. "Is that what this is?"

"I don't know," she murmured. "I guess it could be."

She guessed it could be? And wouldn't that be a perfect ending to a perfect night?

Micah wasn't ready to jump to the sex just yet, though. "Well, why don't we take things slow, see where the night leads us."

Lindy nodded. "Okay, but if it does lead us … there, I want you to know I'm okay with that. I'm not looking for something serious. Well, I mean, not from you." Her face reddened. "God, that sounded terrible. That's not what I meant. I mean, I decided before I met you that I wanted a one-night stand. Then you showed up and I figured—"

Wanting to stop her from rambling, Micah leaned in and pressed his mouth to hers.

Lindy sighed instantly, her lips brushing his softly.

Something in the way she conceded had him pressing his mouth more fully to hers, sliding his tongue along the seam and coaxing her lips apart. When her tongue met his, Micah released a low growl, reminding himself he'd just met her. Taking her right here on this couch probably wasn't a good idea. At least not yet.

However, the night was still young, and based on what she just told him…

Micah was pretty sure this woman was ready and willing to live out her fantasy.

He only hoped she'd be willing to live out his as well.

5

Hayden walked up in time to see Micah lean in and kiss the sexy woman who was sitting beside him. At first he'd been a little awestruck, mesmerized by the sight. A smile had formed at the same time his dick had twitched, hope suddenly coursing through his veins. He hadn't anticipated this tonight, but he wouldn't deny it was a welcome change to his evening plans. Although, if he really thought about it, he hadn't had any plans. Not until Micah had texted him a short time ago and asked him to meet him here.

They came here often. For one, they worked here, and two, they enjoyed the scenery. But to this point, they hadn't utilized the VIP section the way a lot of attendees had. If Micah kept kissing that woman like that, Hayden figured that was about to change.

When Micah pulled back, his full attention still on the fair-skinned woman with the smoking-hot body and sinful black dress, Hayden stepped closer. Both heads turned to look at him, and he instantly saw the heat that glimmered in Micah's dark eyes.

Oh, boy. Hayden wasn't exactly privy to what had taken place thus far, but if that look on Micah's face was anything to go by…

"Lindy Weatherford, I'd like you to meet Hayden Wellington. Hayden, this is Lindy. She came to meet friends, but they aren't here right now."

Had they left already? Or about to show up? Hayden suddenly hoped it was the former.

"Very nice to meet you," he greeted the woman when she smiled up at him.

She looked nervous, but there was something else—determination, maybe?—that glinted in her light blue eyes. And holy shit, her eyes were so pale they were almost colorless. They were intense, especially in a face framed by inky black hair. She was stunning.

Hayden took a seat to Lindy's left, keeping her between him and Micah. He reached for his drink, which Micah had so kindly ordered for him. "I didn't mean to interrupt."

"Oh, you didn't," she said breathlessly. "We were just … uh…"

Resisting the urge to smile, Hayden took a sip of the scotch as he continued to watch the pair. Micah's gaze flipped from Hayden to Lindy, then back. However, Lindy seemed to be avoiding all eye contact. With either of them.

"We were just talking about Lindy's one-night stand."

Lindy dropped her head into her hand and chuckled. "I can't believe I told you that."

Damn, she was cute.

"Do tell," Hayden encouraged, smiling.

Micah met his gaze and offered a nearly imperceptible nod.

"I tend to ramble when I'm nervous," she explained, turning slightly to face him. "I'm an accountant, so we don't have the best social skills, either. Needless to say, I opened my mouth and … well, I don't know why I blurted it out, but I did and…"

31

"I don't mind if you ramble," he told her when she paused, holding her gaze.

She shifted so that she was sitting a little closer to Micah but facing Hayden. He didn't know if that was because she felt safe with Micah or if she merely wanted to look at Hayden when she spoke.

Either way, it was a good sign.

"I seriously just met him a few minutes ago, and I've already put my foot in my mouth."

Hayden looked up at Micah, waiting to see if he would elaborate.

When he didn't, Hayden glanced back at Lindy. "When I walked up, I could've sworn that was his tongue inside that sweet little mouth and not your foot."

Lindy groaned but laughed as she took a deep breath. "I've screwed this up so badly."

"Screwed what up?" Micah asked, leaning down so that his mouth was closer to her ear.

Hayden noticed her nipples tightening behind the silk of her dress. He wanted to slip those thin straps off her arms and suck the hardened points until she was writhing and begging. He wanted to uncover the silky-smooth skin beneath, knowing that every eye in the room would be on her.

32

He refrained.

For now.

"I shouldn't've said what I did."

Now Hayden was curious. Something was clearly going on between these two, and if they really had met only a few minutes ago, Hayden wanted to know how they'd gone from *nice to meet you* to *let's play tonsil hockey* so quickly.

Hayden took another drink. "You'll have to enlighten me, sweetheart. That look on Micah's face says he disagrees."

Lindy shivered, her gaze sliding to Micah over her shoulder, then back. "I told him I wanted him to be my one-night stand. I've never had one."

Hayden liked her. She was sinfully hot but enticingly innocent. And so goddamn beautiful.

"Is that your fantasy?" Micah prompted, still leaning in close to her ear.

Lindy shrugged.

"Want to hear mine?" Micah asked while Hayden continued to watch the two of them closely.

"M-maybe." Lindy reached for her drink.

Micah was kind enough to let her take a sip before he spoke. Hayden already knew what he was going to say to her, and this was going to end one of three ways. Lindy Weatherford was going to freak out and run, or she was going to bombard them with a million questions, or—the best-case scenario—she was going to decide that she might be open to something a little more erotic than a one-night stand with one man.

Her eyes met Hayden's and she seemed to be waiting for something.

"I already know all of his fantasies," Hayden informed her softly, never breaking eye contact.

At first, he could tell she didn't understand his meaning. He continued to study her face, waiting. If her lip curled up, he would know she found that appalling. If it didn't, it would be a safe bet that she would find it interesting.

There was something in Lindy's eyes that told him she was a little tired of the mundane. If he had to guess, she was ready to take a walk on the wild side.

If so, then she was in good hands. Because without a doubt, Hayden and Micah would gladly lead the way.

6

Lindy stared at the sexy newcomer. Hell, she hadn't been able to take her eyes off him since he'd walked up. He carried himself like a man who knew who he was and was comfortable in his own skin. He had the same dark demeanor that Micah had, but there was a glint of humor in his hazel eyes. It was odd that she found herself as attracted to him as she was to Micah.

If anyone would've told her that tonight she'd be practically sandwiched between two of the hottest men to grace the planet, she would've told them to lay off the booze.

But here she was, trying to decipher what Hayden had just said.

I already know all of his fantasies.

Did that mean...? Were they...?

She peered back at Micah, then returned her gaze to Hayden. "I'm not sure … um … what you guys want from me."

And that was true. She was more confused than ever. Based on the way Hayden was looking at her, she was missing a very significant point of this conversation, but she didn't know what it was. Did they think she was a hooker?

Surely not.

"Are you…?" Crap, she didn't even know what she was asking. Once again, she was embarrassed, her face probably as crimson as the lights overhead at this point.

She felt the warmth of Micah's breath against her neck. "Have you ever been with two men, Lindy?"

"At the same time…?" she questioned, realizing how stupid that sounded as soon as the words were out of her mouth.

"At the same time," he confirmed.

"N-no."

She felt the brush of Micah's lips against her skin, and her nipples hardened painfully. Lindy knew she should be freaked out, probably running as fast as she could, but she was glued to her seat, wanting him to elaborate.

"What if I told you that I would like to take you up on your offer?" Micah's words were a deep, seductive whisper. "But I want Hayden to assist me in pleasuring you. Double the intensity, take you places you've never been before.

Lindy found her lungs burning, and she forced herself to take a breath. She was mesmerized by the sound of Micah's voice and the sensual look on Hayden's face.

"Is that what you want?" she found herself asking Hayden.

"Very much."

"Oh." She glanced back at Micah, then over at Hayden. "*Oh!*"

Were they propositioning her to be in a three-way? Holy crap.

Micah's warm body pressed up against her back. Ever since he'd kissed her, Lindy had been hyperaware of him. She didn't know how she'd gotten in this position quite so quickly, either. Not once in her life had she ever dreamed of walking into a club and making out with a man she knew absolutely nothing about.

Okay, so she knew his name. Other than that, she knew nothing.

Not his age.

Not where he lived.

Not where he worked.

Not…

Well, he was clearly interested in a three-way, so that was two things she knew about him.

Oh, and he was one hell of a kisser.

"Do you understand what that means?" Micah whispered.

Lindy shook her head. At this point, it could mean anything.

"We're bisexual," Hayden said, his voice low but easily heard over the sound of the music.

Bisexual? That meant … they both slept with men *and* women. They both wanted to sleep with her and… Oh! They both wanted to sleep with each other, too.

When Micah didn't elaborate, Lindy felt the need to at least say something. "I mean, I know what bisexual means. But I don't know what that means for … me."

She glanced over at Hayden, his hazel eyes still fixed on her face. The smile he offered was nothing short of sinful.

"It means," Micah said softly against her ear, "if you're looking for a one-night stand, it will be with both of us. At the same time."

38

An explosion of warmth detonated in her belly. It was the absolute last thing she expected to feel at this point. Shouldn't she be freaked out? Shouldn't she be running far and fast in the opposite direction?

Then again...

She'd just been thinking about how she wouldn't have any interesting stories to tell her kids. To be fair, this wouldn't be one of those interesting stories she would tell them, but she could tell someone, right? Like Tabitha. Lindy could imagine how that would go:

"Hey, Tabby. Last night, when you stood me up at the club, I met this guy and his..." Was Hayden Micah's partner? Anyway... *"I met this intensely sexy stranger and his friend. And you can no longer call me the humdrum best friend, because I spent the night with both of them."*

Oh, boy. Lindy feared she was losing her mind. How could she even be giving this a second thought?

"Imagine it this way," Micah said, his erotic voice raking over her nerve endings. "We'll slide that pretty little dress off your body, then make you come a million different ways before the sun comes up."

Lindy inhaled sharply, his words causing her clit to pulse with the need to let him do whatever he wanted to do to her. She realized Hayden was staring at her intently, his eyes sparkling with dark promises. He really was incredibly attractive.

"I'm not sure that's a good idea," she forced herself to say. "I don't know you."

That was the truth, at least. She didn't know them.

"We'll tell you anything you want to know," Hayden whispered, leaning in closer.

With Micah at her back and Hayden at her front, Lindy's body coiled tight, but it wasn't from fear. They were in a public place. There was even a bouncer standing a few feet away, guarding their area. Sure, his back was to them, but he would help her if she screamed; she knew that much.

Lindy knew this was crazy. Like, all-time dumbest idea in the world.

Then again … she had been willing to have a one-night stand with a complete stranger. If she got to know these two, she could get two one-night stands in one night. That would definitely make her ineligible for humdrum, and she could easily move on with her life knowing that she'd let loose one night. No holds barred. Without restraint.

Micah's lips pressed against her neck at the same time Hayden leaned in, his breath fanning her lips. They weren't crushing her. She wasn't even sure they were touching her. It seemed more like they were encouraging her to take a walk on the wild side.

She thought about how boring her life had been lately. Work seemed to be her only focus. She hadn't dated in at least eighteen months. In fact, that would've been the last time she had sex, which explained why her hormones were on the fritz right now.

"You just have to say yes," Hayden mumbled, his lips barely brushing hers.

"And we'll take care of the rest," Micah added, his tongue sliding over the sensitive skin of her neck.

"One night?" she asked. "To act out a fantasy?"

"If that's all you want," Micah said. "One night where your pleasure is ours."

"Say yes, Lindy," Hayden encouraged.

Not giving herself time to talk herself out of it, Lindy nodded, then did something she'd never done before. She crushed her mouth to Hayden's and let his tongue explore her mouth the same way she'd allowed Micah only a short time ago.

41

Without Restraint

One night.

All in.

Without restraint.

7

When Lindy kissed Hayden, every one of Micah's nerve endings came roaring to life. Micah's mouth still lingered on her neck, so when Hayden deepened the kiss, he pressed his lips to her skin. She smelled good. Something sweet and musky. It was sexy and exceedingly feminine.

Lindy pulled back from Hayden, then turned her head toward Micah. Her eyes were slightly glazed, her lips wet from Hayden's kiss. Micah took the opportunity presented to him. He swiped his tongue over her lips, tilting his head to get a better angle before diving deeper, plundering her mouth, letting her feel the tension coiling his insides. Her hand slid to his thigh. She was trembling, and he wondered whether that was due to lust or fear. It bothered him enough that he pulled back, giving her some space.

He was all for exploring this woman as far as she would let them, but he wanted her to be comfortable. She was right, they didn't know the first thing about one another. Not that it was a problem. The chemistry between the three of them was enough to set off the smoke alarms, so they could let this play out on desire alone. No doubt, the three of them would walk away completely satisfied.

Only Micah wasn't sure he was going to want to walk away. Certainly not tonight, maybe not ever.

Which, really, was a stupid thing to think about. He didn't know the first thing about this woman. Other than she was sexy and sweet and… From the moment he'd seen her, he'd been intrigued. Enough that he wanted to spend some time getting to know her and allowing her the same opportunity.

Releasing her hip, Micah sat up straight, then reached for her drink and handed it to her. After getting his own, he eased back into the cushions and nodded to Hayden to do the same. They needed to start off slow, take their time.

"So, what did you want to know?" Micah prompted, letting her know they would be moving forward at her pace.

Lindy took a sip, then finally got comfortable between them. From their perch on the couch, they could see the others around them. It was close to eleven, about the time when the place got lively. The Devil's Playground VIP lounge wasn't a place for the timid, that was for sure.

"When you said you know all of his fantasies, what does that mean?" she asked Hayden.

Hayden had already admitted to being bisexual, so Micah figured she was inquiring more about their relationship than whether or not they fucked each other.

"It means we've been together for a while," Hayden admitted.

"Exclusively?"

"Yes."

Lindy looked over at Micah. "So that means you don't have sex with other people?"

Micah shook his head. "Not unless we're together." He didn't tell her that it hadn't happened yet.

"Oh." She lifted her glass to her mouth.

"Which hasn't happened yet," Hayden noted, meeting Micah's gaze, then peering back at Lindy. "It's important that you know that. That you understand this is important to us."

45

For several minutes, the three of them sat there and said nothing, Lindy clearly pondering this new information. Micah didn't know what was going through her mind, but he knew he needed to distract her before she decided to back out. That was definitely her prerogative, but he didn't want to see her leave. Even if they didn't have sex tonight, he wanted to spend more time with her.

After all, there was always that chance that this woman had been placed in his path for a reason. He hadn't thought it possible until the second he'd laid eyes on her. Now, Micah didn't want to take the chance of letting this moment pass him by.

However, since she seemed to be the one fixated on a one-night stand, he figured that was a safe route to take.

When she finished her drink, Micah took the glass. "Would you like another?"

"No. Thank you. I'm good." She didn't sound good. She sounded nervous.

Handing the glass to Hayden, Micah turned to Lindy. "I'm going to fast-track this," he said softly. "I'm thirty-eight. I have a twin brother who manages this club with me. His name is Isaiah. I live here in the hotel in a luxury suite because I work every night of the week. I'm a Libra. My birthday is October sixth. When you walked into the room, I knew this night was going to take a turn for the better. And when Hayden arrived, I knew then that this was right."

Her eyes never strayed from his.

"Is there anything else you want to know, because if not … if you trust me … us … I need to play out one of those fantasies right now."

"Here?" she asked, looking past the sheer curtains that shielded them.

"Right here," he confirmed. "Do you trust me?"

Her eyes caressed his face slowly, then she smiled. "I'm twenty-nine. I have a younger sister who lives in California. I see her on occasion, but we aren't exactly close. I have a small apartment not too far from the strip. I very rarely come down here. I'm an accountant. My birthday is May tenth, and, call me crazy, but yes, I do trust you."

Micah was mesmerized by the sultry sound of her voice. It took him a second to grasp the last part, but when he did, he leaned down and pressed his lips to hers, slowly shifting until his back was in the corner of the sofa and she was sitting in his lap, slightly angled, her back partially against his chest. In an effort to keep from crushing his dick, he moved again so that his rock-hard cock pressed up against her sweet little ass. At this angle, he got a fantastic view of her incredible tits and he still had access to her mouth.

"Your turn," he told Hayden, desperately ready to take this to the next level.

Hayden didn't hesitate with his response. "I'm thirty-four," he said, moving closer.

Micah had moved to the opposite end of the couch, shifting slightly to the side, and managed to get Lindy in his lap, her legs hanging over his thigh, ankles crossed. It would be so easy for Hayden to kneel on the floor, work his way between her legs, to spread her pussy lips with his fingers and bury his tongue in her cunt.

And that would be the route they were taking, he knew it. How, he wasn't sure. Micah was in control here, but they'd been together long enough for Hayden to know that Micah liked to watch. No, they hadn't shared a woman between them yet, but yes, they'd both been with women. And yes, what Micah had told Lindy was true. They hadn't shared a woman between them, and they weren't with anyone else unless they were together. Until now, the other party had simply been a voyeur.

"I live here in the hotel because I'm security for the club, as well as for those who own and manage it. I was born November twentieth, and the only thing I want more than to spend the night driving you absolutely fucking crazy is to spend the night driving you both crazy."

Lindy's eyes flashed with recognition, and he knew she understood this would be more than she'd ever imagined.

"Are you ready to let me play out my fantasy?" Micah whispered into Lindy's ear while holding Hayden's gaze.

"I'm ready," she said, sounding completely sure of herself.

It was Hayden's turn to confirm she was really ready. "If at any time you aren't comfortable, simply say so. That's all I need to hear. Okay, Lindy? This is about you. Your pleasure."

Lindy nodded.

Micah's hand slid down to Lindy's thigh, his palm gliding over her dress before reversing and going back toward her hips, lifting the silky material with his fingers.

"H-here? We're … uh … going to do this here?"

Micah pressed his mouth to her ear. "Right here. Where anyone can watch, and someone probably will. Is that okay with you?"

Lindy looked somewhat perplexed.

"If it's not, say the word," Hayden instructed.

"No … I'm… It's fine."

Hayden's eyes dropped to the spot where Micah's tan fingers continued to drift over her pale, smooth skin. He watched as the dress inched higher, higher still, until he saw the black silk that covered her pussy.

"Okay?" Micah asked.

Lindy nodded, her attention on Micah's hand as well.

"I want to watch Hayden touch you," he told her. "I want to see how hot he makes you."

Another nod was all she offered.

After Hayden put his drink down, he pushed the table out of his way. With one hand on Lindy's thigh, Hayden got down on his knees in front of her, placed his hands on her ankles, then slid them over her shins, her sexy knees, then over her thighs until he met Micah's fingers with his. He took a moment to brush over those powerful hands before dropping his fingers between Lindy's legs, letting his fingertips caress her silk-covered mound.

Lindy inhaled sharply, but she didn't look up at him.

"Do you like that?" Micah asked. "The way he touches you?"

"Yes."

"Do you want him to continue?"

She finally looked up. First at him, then out into the club. Hayden didn't have to look to know that no one was likely watching them. Sure, there could be a voyeur or two who hadn't quite kicked off their own night at this point, but he doubted she would see anyone watching.

The thought alone made his dick swell. The voyeur in him liked the idea of watching and being watched.

Lindy looked back at him. "Yes."

"Does it worry you that someone might be watching?" Micah inquired.

Lindy met Hayden's gaze. "Surprisingly, no." She blinked slowly, as though gathering her thoughts. "I mean … I don't know them. They don't know me."

God, this woman was too fucking perfect.

Hayden caressed her slowly, holding her stare while the wet silk beckoned him. When she slowly spread her legs, he took that as encouragement, allowing his right index finger to slip beneath the elastic edge to find her warm, slick folds beneath.

"Oh, God." Lindy's head fell back against Micah's shoulder.

Hayden locked eyes with Micah, loving the heat he saw reflected there. The man was turned on. The night wouldn't be rushed; he understood that. In fact, he hoped it wasn't, because he didn't want this to be the only night for them.

"Finger her pussy," Micah instructed, his voice low enough that Hayden hardly heard him, but he knew it was more for Lindy's benefit than his.

Without Restraint

Hayden pulled the damp, silky fabric over with his left hand and allowed his index finger to caress her slit, briefly grazing her clit, then slipping lower. He continued to tease her, never stopping to play with her clit, never pushing his finger inside her on the downstroke. He merely brushed over the sensitive nerve endings.

"You want more?" Micah asked.

Lindy nodded.

"Tell him," Micah instructed. "Tell Hayden what you want."

Hayden noticed her chest was heaving as she panted for air. She was turned on and he'd hardly touched her yet. He couldn't wait to bury his tongue in her pussy, to taste her, to feel her clench around his fingers. Most of all, Hayden couldn't wait to make this woman come for the first time.

And then he wanted to spend the rest of the night doing it over and over again.

9

Lindy couldn't believe she was sitting on Micah's lap while Hayden teased her with his finger. She couldn't believe she was in public, where other people could be watching. She also couldn't believe that she was enjoying this more than she'd ever thought possible. But most of all, she couldn't believe that she wanted more.

She wanted everything. Right here with all these people surrounding them, giving in to their own passions, desires. She didn't care where they were, as long as these two men continued to focus their attention on her.

God, she wanted Hayden to slide his finger inside her, to fill the emptiness, to assuage the ache that was consuming her. Lindy figured it wouldn't take much to make her come. Not at this rate anyway. Seriously, eighteen months was a really long time to go without sex. Not that she hadn't used her vibrator during that dry spell, but … it wasn't the same.

And this… Wow. It was beyond hot.

Sure, Lindy couldn't exactly figure out why she was still here. Two men… That wasn't even something she'd ever thought about. Well, that wasn't entirely true. She did have a few secrets, and one of them included reading some rather risqué fiction. Did she ever think she'd be sitting on one man's lap while another looked as though he was ready to have her for dessert?

Um … no. Not in a million years.

So why did she hope that Hayden would continue?

"Tell him, Lindy," Micah whispered in her ear again.

Lindy could feel his hand on her lower back. The tension in his fingers reflected the same knots that she was feeling in every muscle fiber. It was as though she were about to fly apart in a dozen directions.

"I don't know," she rasped. She really didn't. "I want…" God, this was hard. Lindy stared at Hayden's hand between her legs. Finally, she managed to look him in the eye. "Don't stop. Please."

No, maybe it wasn't quite a command, but still. It was something.

When Hayden pulled his hand back, Lindy feared she would cry out from disappointment. Thankfully, he flipped his palm over, and then…

"Oh, my God!" Her head fell back when his finger entered her. The way he curled it so perfectly… "Yes, yes… Oh, God, yes."

Micah's hand slid into her hair, gripping it firmly. There wasn't any pain involved, just a sense of control that sent another shiver racing through her.

"So fucking hot," Micah growled in her ear. "I want Hayden to make you come."

Yes. She wanted that, too. "Please."

Hayden's finger began to move. Slowly at first. In. Out. In. Deeper. Never did he change the pace, and Lindy wished she could force him to hurry up. She was so close.

Micah used his grip on her hair to turn her head so that his mouth was closer to hers. "Damn, sweet girl. I could watch this all night."

Lindy swallowed hard but then gave in to Micah's kiss. Never had a man kissed her quite like this. Micah's lips were firm yet soft. His tongue gentle yet in control. He was as demanding as he was sexy. And still, Lindy couldn't wrap her head around the fact that she was in a public place getting fingered by one sexy man while being thoroughly kissed by another.

When Micah's lips released hers, Lindy drew in air, tilting her head forward again so she could watch Hayden's finger.

"Spread your legs," Micah commanded softly.

Lindy did.

"Make her come with your tongue, Hayden."

Oh, heavens.

Unable to look away, Lindy watched as Hayden leaned in, pulling her panties to the side as his mouth moved closer and closer until...

"Watch him," Micah ordered, his breath warm on her cheek. "This is my fantasy. Watching this man right here do wicked things to your sexy body."

Lindy loved how verbal Micah was. It did all sorts of strange things to her.

But damn, it was hard to focus when Hayden's tongue was caressing her clit like that. Almost whisper-soft as he learned what she enjoyed.

Lindy instinctively reached for his head, wanting to pull him closer, but stopped herself. Micah obviously realized what she'd been about to do, because he took her wrist and placed her hand in Hayden's silky brown hair.

"Do it," Micah said, his voice still incredibly low, gentle even. "Show him what you like."

Her hands were trembling, but Lindy managed to twine her fingers in Hayden's dark hair, pulling him closer as she leaned back a little, spreading her legs wider.

"Yes," she hissed when he wrapped his lips around her clit and flicked the extremely sensitive bundle of nerves with his tongue. "Oh, yes... Hayden..."

"Tell us," Micah insisted. "Tell us when you come, Lindy."

Well, that did it. Between Hayden's exquisite tongue and Micah's seductive commands, Lindy couldn't hold out any longer.

"I'm..." Heaven help her, she was never going to forget this night. "Gonna..." Oh, please, don't let it be over after this. "Come!"

Without Restraint

And she did.

10

Micah was three seconds away from pulling out his dick and thrusting it into Hayden's willing mouth. Somehow he managed to wrangle a measure of restraint. It wasn't fucking easy. He damn sure didn't intend to be selfish tonight. Not when he had a smorgasbord in front of him. Between Lindy and Hayden... Fuck, Micah wasn't sure he'd ever been good enough in his lifetime to deserve this.

One thing he did know was that they couldn't continue this right here.

As much as he loved the fact that other people watched—he was a voyeur, tried and true—he needed to get Lindy and Hayden alone. For two reasons. One, he wanted to give Lindy a little time to recover and to ensure that she was still willing to do this. And two, he needed some time to cool off himself before they moved this to the next level.

His twin would be the first to say that patience wasn't Micah's strong suit, but he was drawing on every ounce he possessed.

After Hayden adjusted Lindy's panties, then got to his feet, Micah reached for him, pulling him down and crushing his mouth to Hayden's. To his utter shock, Lindy's hand slid into Micah's hair, and he opened his eyes, noticing she was watching them kiss.

For half a second, he didn't dare breathe, not sure what she was going to say.

Her smile reflected the excitement in her eyes. "Don't stop on my account. I'm finding that I like to watch, too," she told them, then turned Micah's head so that he was once again facing Hayden.

Again, Micah kissed the man, sucking his tongue, savoring the taste of Lindy and Hayden mixed together. He could easily get addicted to this.

Hayden was the one to pull back, his eyes locked with Micah's. Everything the man was feeling—lust, passion, need—was burning brightly in his green-brown gaze. Damn, he wished they were all three naked.

"How about we take this somewhere more private?" Hayden suggested, his eyes sliding toward Lindy.

"I'd like that."

After Hayden helped Lindy up, Micah adjusted himself and got to his feet. He grabbed his phone as he followed the pair out of the club and into the hotel proper. It took ten minutes for them to get up to Micah's room, and during that time, he called and ordered room service. If things went the way he hoped, they would be hungry at some point.

"This is where you live?" Lindy inquired when they stepped inside.

"It is," Micah confirmed.

He couldn't deny that the place was nice. It was, after all, a luxury suite. However, it wasn't home, simply a place for Micah to sleep. Since Sin City never slept, Micah rarely did, either. Sure, he had a day off from time to time, but since his life had been lacking in most areas, work was the only thing he usually focused on.

Well, work and Hayden. These days, anyway.

"Can I get you a drink?" Hayden offered Lindy.

Good. At least one of them was remembering his manners. Micah was still thinking about Hayden fingering Lindy back at the club. Then Hayden lapping at her pussy and making her turn to fire in Micah's arms.

"I'll take water," Lindy told him.

Micah peered over at her to see she was staring back at him. He couldn't begin to imagine what she was thinking.

While Hayden veered into the kitchenette, Micah took Lindy's hand and led her to the small sofa. "Come here, sweet girl. Let me touch you for a few minutes." He noticed the way her eyes widened. "Just touch, I promise."

Micah took off his suit jacket and laid it over the arm of the sofa before taking a seat and pulling Lindy down with him. At the same time, the lights in the room dimmed and the heavy drapes on the floor-to-ceiling windows began inching back, revealing the Las Vegas Strip in all its glittering glory.

Although he spent very little time outside of the walls of the club or the hotel, Micah loved the view from right here. He could sit here for hours, drinking it all in, never getting tired of it.

"It's beautiful," Lindy whispered. "It's funny. I've lived here for a decade. I rarely come down here, but I've always enjoyed this view."

"Me, too," he told her softly.

There was a soft knock on the door, followed by Hayden's quiet, "I'll get it."

Lindy peered up at him in question.

"Room service. That way we have something on hand for later."

She nodded, her gaze sliding back out the windows.

Micah couldn't resist gliding his hands up Lindy's arms, curling his fingers over her collarbone, then skimming lower, his fingertips dipping beneath the silk so he could touch soft, smooth skin.

Lindy sighed, leaning back against him.

He took that as a signal for him to continue, so he did. Micah knew the room service attendant was somewhere behind him, putting the food out on the table, but he didn't care. The man wouldn't be able to see much, if anything. However, the mere thought of someone watching set his blood on fire. He dipped his fingers lower, pushing his hands apart, which forced the thin straps of her dress to fall from her shoulders.

"You have nice hands," she whispered.

"You have amazing tits," he replied, keeping his voice low, directed at her. "So fucking sweet."

She wasn't wearing a bra, which he found intensely erotic, allowing him to glide his hands lower, nothing hindering his progress. With the silk pooling beneath her breasts, Micah continued to fondle her, lightly plucking her nipples while cupping her softly. He let his mouth trail over her jaw, her neck, inhaling her sweet scent. No doubt about it, he was enjoying the hell out of himself.

He heard Hayden dismiss the attendant, then a second later, he was taking a seat in the chair across from them.

Only then did Micah feel complete.

11

Hayden couldn't take his eyes off the pair. The way Micah's big hands caressed Lindy's creamy flesh, her pale nipples pebbled from his touch. She looked relaxed, leaning back against him, her eyes hooded as she succumbed to the pleasure.

"Are you … uh … going to join us?"

"In a minute," he assured her. "I'm good right now. I like to watch."

"Oh."

"Stand up, sweet girl," Micah instructed, his voice low, gentle.

When Lindy got to her feet, Hayden admired her long legs, her sweet curves. She was so damn pretty.

Micah easily worked the dress down over the flare of her hips and let it pool on the floor at her feet. Lindy stepped out of the silk, seemingly comfortable standing there in the sexy heels and a mind-numbing black thong. Her breasts were full and high, her light pink nipples mouthwateringly sexy.

"Come back down here," Micah crooned, tugging on her arm until she was once again perched on his lap.

Hayden slid his hand over his throbbing cock, trying to offer some relief. If this went on for too long, no way would he be able to avoid taking himself in hand.

Once again, Lindy was watching out the window while Micah trailed his hands over her skin, sliding down the gentle curve of her belly, stopping at the apex of her thighs before heading back up. He was teasing her, Hayden knew, and based on the way Lindy's eyes closed briefly, she was enjoying every second of it.

"I need to taste you," Micah told her, his fingers tugging on the hardened points of her nipples. "Can I taste you, Lindy? Put my mouth right here?"

"Yes," she murmured on a soft moan. "God, yes."

Her voice was throaty and sexy, making Hayden's dick jump.

"Will you come over here now?" Lindy asked, her question directed at him.

"I'll do anything you want me to do," he informed her. And it was true. Tonight was about her.

Hayden got to his feet and removed his jacket, laying it on the back of the chair. He removed the cuff links on his shirt and rolled his sleeves up, trying to get more comfortable.

Micah shifted so that Lindy was reclining on his lap, her back against the arm of the sofa. When Micah's head dipped down, his tongue sliding over her nipple, Hayden's dick twitched. Dropping to his knees on the floor before them, Hayden took her other nipple in his mouth.

"Oh…" Lindy's head dropped back, her breast jutting up, offering herself to them.

It was so damn sexy, almost completely innocent, except for the way her fingers tangled in his hair, pulling him closer.

"You taste so damn good, sweet girl," Micah mumbled.

When Micah shifted again, spreading his legs wider, Hayden moved so that he was between Micah's knees. While he laved Lindy's breast, nipping her gently, he tucked his hand beneath her so he could graze Micah's cock.

A soft growl rumbled in Micah's chest as he lifted his head.

Hayden met his eyes, knew what he wanted, but refused to give it to him until he asked. He would do anything for the man, anything at all. Micah simply had to tell him what he wanted, what he needed.

Lindy was watching them both, probably seeing every ounce of need etched on each of their faces. Hayden looked down at her, then leaned in and pressed his lips to hers, inhaling her sigh, sucking on her tongue, trying to rein himself in. Micah was setting the pace, and Hayden liked the direction this was going. A slow seduction was just what the three of them needed. It would be torturous but worth it in the end.

When Hayden released her mouth, Lindy pulled Micah's head down, kissing him while Hayden watched. There was something about Micah, something so damn sexy it was often hard to look at him. The way he kissed Lindy reflected his control, his desire to draw this out, to make it good for all three of them.

Rather than get too far ahead of himself, Hayden returned his attention to Lindy, sliding his mouth over her collarbone, her breast, then down her belly. He could feast on her for hours if she'd let him. He kept himself in check, making sure he limited himself to touching her only. He'd heard what Micah told her, and he was more than willing to play by the man's rules.

He knew from experience, Micah's rules would draw out the pleasure and give him all that he needed. He simply had to be patient.

Sometimes that was easier said than done.

12

Lindy wasn't sure what she'd expected when she agreed to come back to Micah's room, but this surely wasn't it. This sweet seduction was quickly going to her head, making her want things she'd never before wanted.

Although she knew she should feel awkward with two men touching her, kissing her, she didn't. Not in the least. It seemed natural, the way the two men worked in tandem to please her. The soft words they whispered only made her burn hotter; the way their strong, gentle hands caressed her body made her want more.

She had never been the adventurous type, certainly not when it came to sex. Her experience was limited and relatively decent. The men she'd been with had always tried to do what they thought she wanted. Until now, she hadn't realized that this was what she wanted. To give herself completely up to someone. Or two some *ones* as was the case. She liked that they held all the control yet they weren't arrogant and demanding.

"We need more room," Micah purred against her ear. "I want to lay you out and feast on you for hours. Will you let me, sweet girl? Let me and Hayden make you come?"

She nodded. "Anything," she whispered, wanting him to know that she was a willing and eager participant. Not only did she want to experience all that they were offering to give her but she wanted to explore as well, to live this moment to the fullest.

Hayden retreated before getting to his feet. She hardly had time to catch her breath before he reached down and lifted her into his arms. No one had ever picked her up like this before. She knew she wasn't a lightweight, had always battled the scale. Her job didn't involve anything more than sitting at her desk all day long. She tried to get exercise, she focused on eating healthy, but she still had more cushion on her hips and her belly than she would've liked. Neither man seemed to be turned off by it, so she wasn't about to dwell on it, either.

She wrapped her arms around Hayden's neck as he carried her into the bedroom. Once again, the lights dimmed and the drapes drew back, allowing an enticing view of the strip even from the bedroom. It was both sexy and romantic, adding to the erotic ambience of the evening.

Hayden deposited her on the bed, coming down over her, his mouth fusing with hers. She liked the way he kissed her. His mouth wasn't as soft as Micah's, but equally skilled. His kiss was slightly different, not quite so demanding as his tongue stroked hers. Lindy found she liked the subtle differences between the two men.

A muted growl sounded from beside her, and when Hayden pulled back, she noticed Micah stretched out beside them. She watched his face, his eyes. The way he looked at Hayden told her these two men were intimately close. When she'd seen them kissing down in the club, it had stoked a fire inside her, burning her with flames that quickly intensified. She'd never seen something so sexy in her life.

Glancing up at Hayden, she saw him watching Micah. She knew he wanted to go to him, and honestly, she wanted to watch as well.

"Let me watch for a minute," she suggested, glancing between the two men.

They both glanced at her momentarily before she urged Hayden closer to Micah by pressing against his hip.

"I like the way you think," he told her, the dark cadence of his voice washing over her.

Hayden crawled over her, moving closer to Micah. He looked to be on the hunt, ready to devour his prey. Her pussy clenched, her clit throbbing with an ache she was becoming increasingly familiar with as the night progressed.

When Hayden draped himself over Micah, her breath caught in her throat. They were masculine and sexy, and watching them together was an assault on the senses.

75

"Fuck yes," Micah hissed, grabbing Hayden and yanking him closer, their mouths crushing together.

Lindy leaned up on one elbow, sliding her hand over Hayden's back, his shoulder, then touching Micah. She didn't want to interrupt, content to simply watch, but she wanted to touch them, to feel the energy their bodies generated when they came together.

Their kiss didn't last as long as she'd hoped, but they obviously weren't finished. Hayden rolled off Micah, lying on his other side. Micah then reached for her, pulling her close until their mouths touched. She was kissing him, his smooth hand gliding over her back, her butt, her thighs. Hayden leaned in, and suddenly the three of them were kissing, taking turns, mouths searching, seeking, pleasuring.

When she'd walked into the club tonight, she had agreed to a one-night stand. Never in her life would she have imagined this. Never would she have known that there could be so much more.

Lindy only hoped that by the time the night was over, she'd be willing to go back to the mundane world she lived in knowing that these two men were out there and she wasn't going to be a part of it.

13

This was surreal. Lying here, kissing Hayden and Lindy felt better than anything Micah had ever known before. He knew what to expect from Hayden; the man did things to him that he hadn't expected to ever feel, but having Lindy with them made him feel whole, as though the circuits within him were completed.

And to think, they were just getting started.

While his mouth lingered with Lindy's, he felt Hayden's fingers working the buttons on his shirt, the warmth of his hand as it slid over his chest, his stomach. He wanted them all naked, wanted to feel them skin to skin. Thankfully, Hayden seemed to be on board with that plan.

Lindy pulled her mouth from his, letting her lips trail over his jaw, his neck. Her tongue lingered on his skin, leaving sparks of heat in its wake. She seemed to be following Hayden's hands. Every button that opened, her mouth trailed lower. He finally succumbed to the onslaught, lifting his hands behind his head, allowing himself room to watch them.

Hayden's eyes met his, and there was a wealth of communication in the look. Micah simply nodded once, letting Hayden know this was exactly what he wanted, what they both needed. The heat that ignited in Hayden's eyes, the green nearly overtaking the brown, made him suck in air. He'd never seen Hayden this hot before, this needy.

"Oh, fuck," Micah hissed when Lindy's smooth fingers dipped beneath the waistband of his slacks, her fingertips grazing the swollen head of his cock. "Touch me, sweet girl. I want to feel your hands all over me."

She continued to kiss his stomach while working his belt open, then lifted her head while Hayden replaced her mouth with his. The differences between them were dramatic. Hayden was all hard muscle and sleek angles to Lindy's soft, smooth curves. Micah watched, fascinated as the two of them worked his pants open, then removed them from his body. He helped them along by unhooking the cuffs on his shirt and discarding it as well. When he was lying there completely naked, both of their eyes slowly raking over him, all the blood in his body rushed to his dick, making it throb painfully.

"Oh, God, touch me," he growled. "Someone fucking touch me."

Lindy's cool hand slid up the inside of his thigh while Hayden wrapped his fingers around Micah's cock, stroking him.

Micah forced his eyes to remain open, not wanting to miss a second. He drew air into his lungs with slow, deep breaths, biting the inside of his cheek when Lindy's fingers grazed his balls. It took tremendous effort to keep his hands behind his head when the only thing he wanted to do was grab Hayden's head and pull his mouth down to his dick.

It came in time. That sweet fucking tongue swiped over the engorged head, licking him while Hayden met his gaze.

"God, yes. Suck me." His eyes rolled to the back of his head when Hayden took him all the way to the root. "Oh, fuck yes. So good. Love your mouth. Fucking love your mouth."

Micah opened his eyes to see Lindy observing intently, her hand sliding over her own thigh. Reaching for her, Micah pulled her back down to him, kissing her lips while the warm suction of Hayden's mouth made his dick throb and pulse. Her hand never stopped roaming over him, as though she was as eager to touch as they were. She didn't balk at the fact that Hayden had Micah's dick in his mouth. In fact, it seemed to turn her on, a fact she couldn't hide when she ground her pussy against Micah's thigh.

"You like this, sweet girl?" he whispered.

"So much." Her breath fanned his lips. "I want to taste you, too."

Micah groaned low in his throat. Hayden must've heard her, too, because he pulled back, his fist still wrapped tightly around Micah's shaft.

"Come here," Hayden urged. "Put your mouth on him, Lindy."

Micah wasn't prone to premature ejaculation, but holy fucking hell. He could usually go for hours before he reached the pinnacle of release, but if she kept doing that wicked thing with her tongue, all bets were off.

"Naked," Micah commanded Hayden. "I want you naked."

Hayden climbed off the bed and slowly undressed, watching as Lindy laved Micah's dick. It was evident she was shy, not completely skilled in giving head, but she made up for her lack of experience with sheer enthusiasm.

Micah was all for letting them tease him, but he wanted to give in return. He wanted to feel Hayden's cock between his lips, taste the sweetness of Lindy's pussy on his tongue.

Reaching out for Hayden, Micah urged him back onto the bed, guiding him up near his head so he could return the favor.

14

After discarding his clothes, Hayden palmed his cock, stroking slowly while he watched Lindy bob up and down on Micah's dick. She seemed lost in the moment, completely focused on pleasuring him.

It wasn't until Micah reached for him that Hayden realized he'd been standing there for too long.

"Put your dick in my mouth," Micah insisted, his smoldering gaze locking with Hayden's. "Let me do to you what she's doing to me."

Oh, hell, yes.

Hayden returned to the bed, kneeling beside Micah's head so as not to completely obstruct his view. The first touch of Micah's tongue on his cock made him light-headed. Hayden slid his fingers into Micah's hair, holding his head while he pushed past Micah's lips, forcing himself deeper into the man's mouth.

Lindy looked up, her small hand still wrapped around Micah's thick cock, her eyes widening.

"Come up here," Hayden instructed. "Put your sweet lips on my dick, too. I want to feel both of you."

Micah shifted down the mattress, flattening himself out, while Lindy moved up on his other side. When Micah pulled back, she sucked Hayden into the furnace of her mouth, sucking him lightly, gently. Every cell in his body was on fire, a desperate, aching need sweeping through him.

"Heaven … have … mercy…" Hayden gripped Micah's hair tighter when the man sucked Hayden's balls into his mouth while Lindy kept her lips wrapped firmly around the head. Two mouths on him was exquisite, more than he'd ever imagined.

Lindy moaned around his cock, sending shards of electricity forking through his entire body, making his skin tingle.

When Micah released his balls, their eyes met, and Hayden knew it was time to switch. Time to show this sexy woman exactly what they had in store for her. As much as Hayden enjoyed what she was doing to him, he wanted to spend the rest of the night making her cry out in ecstasy, driving her to the brink of sexual insanity and then back again.

He allowed Micah to guide her mouth back to his, giving Hayden a moment to catch his breath. He watched as Micah focused all his attention on Lindy, pulling her on top of him, cupping the back of her head while he feasted on her mouth. Hayden retrieved condoms and lube from the nightstand drawer and tucked them beneath the pillow so they'd have them when they needed them before returning to the bed, this time to the end.

He positioned himself between Micah's legs, sliding his chest over Lindy's lush ass. She wiggled against him, urging him higher. Kissing her hip, her back, all the way up her spine, he didn't stop until she was practically crushed between them. His cock grazed her ass and he fought for air once more. The mental image of her between them, his dick in her ass while Micah fucked her pussy, made his heart skip a beat.

He soothed his raging libido by assuring himself they would get there. Eventually.

But right now, he wanted to taste her again.

Micah seemed to know exactly what he wanted. Hayden shifted over, allowing Micah to roll Lindy onto her back, their lips brushing as he did. Hayden watched, his mouth watering with the need to be included. When Micah pulled back, Hayden waited patiently. But then Micah was on him, kissing him, fucking his mouth with his tongue. It was hot and brutal, the complete opposite of how he'd been with Lindy. It was right then that Hayden understood what Micah needed. He needed Hayden to take control, to give him what Hayden knew Micah required while he took from Lindy, pleasuring her. Micah wanted both gentle and sweet, rough and easy. And having both of them would give the man exactly that.

It all made sense.

And it mirrored exactly what Hayden desired as well.

"I've got you," he whispered to Micah when he pulled back. "Let me take care of you tonight. Both of you."

Micah nodded, then kissed him again before turning his attention to Lindy.

"I'm going to make you come, sweet girl. With my mouth."

Her eyes widened when Micah grabbed her legs, tugging her down on the bed. She smiled. "I thought you'd never ask."

"I'm done asking, sweet girl. I'm going to make you beg."

Another smile tugged at her lips, and if she was at all surprised by Micah's gravel-laced tone, she didn't show it.

"Yeah," she whispered, "I got the feeling you were holding something back."

Hayden pulled her panties down her legs, then straddled her calf while Micah straddled the other, forcing her legs wider.

"You ready for this, sweet girl?" Micah asked.

Lindy's pale blue eyes glowed brightly. "I thought you were done asking."

Micah barked a laugh and Hayden chuckled.

Looked as though the sweet girl had a sassy side.

Hayden was certainly looking forward to more of that.

A lot more.

15

Lindy wasn't sure when she got to be so daring, but she liked the result. And it was true, she had sensed that Micah was holding back. The man was darkly seductive, but underneath that gentle, smooth façade, she sensed a passion that he kept leashed.

Maybe she was playing with fire, but she wanted it all tonight. She wanted everything they would give her. She wasn't one to regret her decisions, and she certainly wasn't regretting what they'd done so far. But, yes, there was a slightly selfish side of herself that wanted them to give her an unforgettable orgasm, to make her body burn hotter than it was already. Then again, if they turned her on anymore, she wasn't sure she'd survive it.

"Close your eyes," Micah instructed.

Lindy instantly closed her eyes, focusing on the feel of them. They were straddling her calves; she could feel the coarse hair on their legs against her skin, their firm hands sliding slowly up her thighs. The sensation was foreign yet not at all unpleasant. Knowing there were two men touching her, four hands caressing her, took some time getting used to. It wasn't the norm, but it didn't necessarily feel taboo. For whatever reason—maybe she was chemically flawed or merely different from most women—it felt right.

When they reached the apex of her thighs, Lindy peeked.

"Keep 'em closed, Lindy," Hayden rumbled. "Or we'll blindfold you."

She closed her eyes again, sucking in a breath when their thumbs slid over her mound, their fingers traveling over the ticklish spot at the tops of her thighs.

"I want to taste you." Micah's voice was laced with hunger. "I want to fuck your pussy with my tongue."

Chill bumps burst out along her skin. She loved his voice, the way he said what he wanted. It was dark and dirty and ... lascivious. Lindy wanted more. Who knew this wanton woman was beneath the ill-fitting suits and the number-crunching nature? She certainly hadn't.

As Hayden and Micah gently massaged her with their fingers, she fought to keep her eyes closed. It wasn't easy when she wanted to watch what they were doing to her.

"Oh," she moaned, the sound ripping up her throat when she felt the warm rasp of a tongue along her slit.

And then there were two tongues, one working her clit, the other teasing her nipple. Sensations assaulted her, firing beneath her skin, along every nerve ending.

When a finger penetrated her, Lindy's back arched, her body silently pleading for more.

"So wet." That was Hayden's voice, deep and low, reverberating through her.

The mouths shifted, her other nipple pebbling from the onslaught while her pussy clenched, desperate for something to fill her. Another finger probed her, pushing in deeper this time. The thick intrusion had her inner muscles clenching, her hands fisting at her sides.

"Let me watch," she pleaded.

"Open your eyes," Micah instructed.

Lindy did, finding both men still hovering over her, their mouths working her into a frenzy.

Another finger penetrated her, along with the first, and when Micah lifted his head from between her thighs, she realized both men were fingering her. They watched her while she watched them.

"More?" Micah's question was as probing as his finger.

"Yes," she whispered. "Everything."

Their fingers worked inside her as they sat up, stroking themselves. She couldn't take her eyes off of them, her body fueled by the visual assault. Two voracious men set out to torment her until her body shattered. Lindy didn't think she could take much more, but then Micah shifted, pulling her up as he fell onto the bed.

"Sit on my face," he commanded. "Let me eat that sweet pussy."

His pupils were dark and dilated, the hard lines etched on his face proof that he was holding on to his control.

Without thinking, she moved over him, her pussy hovering above his face. A rumbled vibration teased her clit, and she glanced over her shoulder to see Hayden taking Micah's cock into his mouth, working him roughly while Micah lapped at her, licking, sucking, fucking with his tongue. Her body hummed, a lightning storm erupting in her core. She couldn't hold back any longer. When he flicked his tongue over her clit, she pressed against his mouth, moaning loudly as she gripped the headboard just as her body splintered, her orgasm hurtling through her, stealing her breath.

Somehow she managed to move off him, wanting to watch Hayden, to see Micah's dick tunneling in and out of his mouth. The man wasn't gentle, but clearly that was what Micah needed. When Micah grabbed Hayden's hair, his fingers tightening in the light brown strands, she heard Hayden's groan, knew he didn't want to stop, but Micah forced him to.

There was a brief lull, but it didn't last long, and for that, Lindy was grateful. Without them touching her, she already felt her need ratcheting up. She wanted one of them inside her, wanted to be fucked hard and fast.

And she wanted it right now.

16

Micah was losing his restraint. He couldn't hold back any longer. He needed to fuck, needed to bury himself inside Hayden. He wanted to fuck Lindy, but he feared he would hurt her. He'd held back too long, his need too great.

Hayden seemed to know what he needed, reaching beneath the pillow and retrieving two condoms. With practiced ease, Hayden sheathed them both, teasing Micah in the process, forcing him to hover closer to the edge of insanity before he produced the lubricant.

"Need to fuck your ass," Micah growled, making sure Hayden was on the same page.

With hands only slightly gentler than Micah's would've been, Hayden reached for Lindy, pulling her beneath him before positioning himself over her body.

"Inside you ... that's the only place I want to be, Lindy," Hayden groaned. "Want to feel your pussy grip my cock."

"Yes," she pleaded. "Please."

Micah gritted his teeth as he lubed his cock, moving behind Hayden as the man pushed inside Lindy's welcoming cunt. God, he wanted to feel her, too, but he knew that would have to wait. Right now, he needed hard and fast. No way could she handle him in this state.

"Can't be easy," he warned Hayden.

Hayden pumped his hips, filling Lindy. Her throaty moans floated in the air, causing Micah's need to ramp up significantly. Watching Hayden fuck her was a sight he'd never tire of. The way her legs wrapped around Hayden's narrow hips, her fingernails digging into Hayden's muscular back.

Micah couldn't wait any longer. He grabbed Hayden's hips, stilling him momentarily as he pushed his cock deep inside him, hoping like hell he had enough resolve not to hurt him.

"Fuck me," Hayden roared. "Fuck me, now."

Lindy's fingernails dug deeper into Hayden's back when Micah began thrusting his hips, drilling Hayden's ass, forcing him deeper into her. The motion of Micah's hips was the momentum Hayden used to drill into her.

"Harder," Lindy begged. "More … please…"

Her soft cry rang in Micah's ears as he continued to plow Hayden's ass, fucking him harder, deeper.

Hayden groaned, his pleasure filling Micah's senses, pulling him closer to release, that point of no return. His skin felt too small for his body, his balls drawing up tight, his scalp tingling from the sensations rocking him. It was too fucking good, better than he'd ever imagined.

"Gonna come," Micah warned. "Can't hold back. Come for us, sweet girl. Come all over Hayden's dick so I can fill his ass."

Lindy cried out, her body jerking. Micah could feel it through Hayden's body. She was coming, the sound so fucking sweet it triggered his own release. His cock twitched and jerked inside Hayden's ass, a feeling so intense, so beautifully fucking brutal he was fairly certain his heart would simply stop beating.

"Fuck yes," Hayden bellowed. "Coming."

Micah fought to breathe, falling over Hayden, relying on him to keep them from crushing Lindy beneath them both. He kissed Hayden's neck, savoring his warmth.

And when Hayden whispered, "I've got you. I've got you both," Micah's heart filled to overflowing. He knew in that moment that this…

This was what he'd always needed, what he'd always wanted. But he knew that it wouldn't happen with just anyone.

And now, he needed to figure out what that meant for all three of them.

17

Sunday morning

As usual, Hayden slept lightly, waking when he felt Lindy move against him. Following the incredible orgasms from the night before, Lindy had drifted off between him and Micah after they'd cleaned up with a quick yet highly erotic shower and had a little late-night snack.

Also as usual, as soon as his eyes opened, Hayden's dick was wide awake as well, eager for a replay of the night before.

"Shh," Micah whispered, drawing Hayden's attention to him.

Hayden glanced over to see Micah kissing Lindy, his mouth seductively sliding over her lips, his tongue stroking in and out of her mouth. Damn, that was a sight to see first thing in the morning. Apparently Micah thought Hayden could sleep through that. No chance in hell.

Moving closer, he pressed up against Lindy's back. She giggled softly, pulling away from Micah and turning to face him.

"Good morning." Her voice was raspy and sexy from sleep.

"Morning," he greeted, staking claim on her lips instantly.

She rolled to her back, giving him better access to her mouth, also allowing him to slide his hands over all that smooth skin, currently covered by the sheet. Hayden pulled it off of her, revealing her delicious body to their hungry gazes.

Her back bowed, causing Hayden to pull back. He found Micah shouldering her thighs apart, his mouth hovering above her pussy, his eyes glazed with heat and desire.

"Ready for round two?" Hayden asked, turning his attention back to her.

"I'm not sure I'll survive it."

"Oh, you will, I promise."

While Micah made Lindy moan with his mouth, Hayden retrieved two more condoms and the bottle of lube. He quickly donned one himself, unable to wait. He wanted to relive last night, but this time, he wanted to feel Lindy crushed between them, the heat of her body engulfing them both at the same time.

When he caught Micah's gaze, he lifted one eyebrow. Micah's dark eyes glittered, and a seductive grin tugged at the corners of his mouth. The man was certainly on board with his plan.

"What are you boys plotting?" Lindy asked, pushing up on her elbows.

Micah crawled over her, pressing her into the mattress as he slid one arm beneath her. In one quick move, he rolled them both so that he was on his back and Lindy was draped over him.

"Put the condom on me," Micah instructed Lindy.

Her grin was sweet and sexy. She seemed to like Micah's bossy side. Hayden knew the feeling. He happened to enjoy it as well.

Lindy retrieved the condom from Hayden's hand and managed to roll it over Micah's length. She took her time, though. Whether that was because she was nervous or simply trying to torment the poor guy, Hayden didn't know. But Micah seemed to enjoy it, nonetheless.

"Come here, sweet girl," Micah crooned softly. "It's my turn to feel your pussy gripping my dick, dragging my sanity right from my body."

Lindy leaned forward and guided Micah inside her before coming to rest over him, straddling his hips.

Hayden flipped open the lube, applied a generous amount to his latex-covered cock before slicking his fingers.

He started by kissing Lindy's shoulders, her back, moving slowly lower as Micah held her against him, his hips rocking gently beneath her. He was taking his time, prepping her, distracting her.

"Do you trust us, Lindy?" Micah grumbled against her ear, his eyes meeting Hayden's.

"Yes," she whispered, wiggling atop him.

"We want to take you at the same time," Hayden told her, sliding his hand up to cup her breast, pinching her nipple lightly. "Can you take both of us?"

She shook her head. "I ... don't know."

Hayden nipped her earlobe gently. "I'll be easy, I promise. I won't hurt you."

"Promise?"

"I swear it," he assured her.

She turned her head, and Hayden couldn't resist kissing her, sliding his tongue against hers while he allowed his fingers to drift down between the rounded globes of her ass. He gently massaged her rosebud, grazing the sensitive skin there until she was breathing hard and rocking back and forth on Micah's cock.

Hayden liked that she was willing, eager even. More importantly, he liked that she trusted them. It couldn't be easy for her, he knew.

When Micah nodded, Hayden began an all-out sensual assault, continuing to trail his lips over Lindy's back while prodding her asshole open with one finger. He fucked her gently, allowing her to acclimate to the intrusion. She was so damn tight, her muscles clamping on his finger with every breath she took.

"Relax, sweet girl," Micah whispered, his voice low. "Does it hurt?"

"No." She moaned softly when Hayden added another finger. "It's … different."

Micah cupped the back of her head, pulling her face back to his. "Let us make you feel good."

Sweat beaded on Hayden's forehead, but he held on to the tight leash on his control. He damn sure wouldn't hurt this woman. She was giving them the ultimate gift, the one thing they both fantasized about.

Could they make her feel good? Absolutely.

Could they let her walk away after this? That was the question Hayden didn't yet have an answer for.

18

Lindy held her breath, trying to relax. The two things seemed to be at war with one another. The only time she felt the tension drain from her body was when Micah kissed her. He was the perfect distraction, and he felt like heaven inside her.

"Breathe for me, sweet girl," Micah mumbled in her ear. "Your pussy's gripping me like a fist."

Exhaling and inhaling, Lindy focused on the warmth of Hayden's hand on her hip, on how gentle he'd been thus far. She couldn't believe she was doing this. In fact, she couldn't believe she was still here. She had always believed that a one-night stand was simply that. One night. Not the next morning.

But here she was, sandwiched between these two men. The same men she'd slept between in the wee hours of the morning. When she had opened her eyes to find them wrapped around her in the bed, Lindy couldn't deny she'd felt safe. Surprised, yes, but also safe with them.

Which was why she trusted them. They'd taken care of her last night, given her something she'd never imagined. Not just the orgasms but also the reminder that she was desirable.

The pressure against her bottom intensified, and she once again held her breath.

"Look at me," Micah ordered, his voice rough, his tone demanding.

She glanced down at him, gazing into his liquid dark eyes.

"Sweet girl…" He lowered his voice. "Do you know how hard it is not to fuck you right now? Not to pound your sweet pussy from beneath, to make you beg me to let you come?"

She swallowed hard, his dirty words penetrating the slight bite of pain.

"It's hell. I want your wet, warm cunt milking my dick."

Lindy squeezed her inner muscles, continuing to watch his face.

"Aww, God. Just like that. I could stay like this forever, right here inside you."

She didn't want to admit it, but she could, too. During the past eight hours, Lindy had found herself immersed in a world she hadn't even known existed, ensconced by pleasure that was out of this world.

"Fuck, baby," Hayden groaned from behind her. "Your ass is so fucking tight. So hot."

When the pain intensified, Micah reached for her head, jerking her down to him, fusing their mouths together as he began moving beneath her, rocking his hips, pushing his cock deeper. Her nerve endings flared, and for a moment, she didn't know where they ended and she began. She felt so full, completely overwhelmed by both of them.

"Just stay like that, sweet girl," Micah whispered against her mouth. "Let us do all the work."

She swallowed hard, trying to process his words. It only took a moment to understand what he meant, because they both started moving. Inside her. At the same freaking time.

There was no pain, only tremendous pressure.

"I feel him," Micah said. "I feel him inside you. This is pure fucking heaven. Better than my ultimate fantasy. So fucking much better."

They both started moving faster, hard hands gripping her hips, pushing and pulling as they fucked her into oblivion. Spasms racked her body; sensations invaded her nerve endings. Electrical pulses detonated, ricocheting from inside her, darting out in all directions. Lindy was coming apart at the seams. She could feel it. Every grunt that echoed from them spurred her forward, driving her closer and closer to release.

"Sweet girl, you feel so fucking good. I can't hold on. Want to come…"

Lindy knew he was holding back because of her, but she didn't care. She was riding the waves of bliss, letting them propel her higher and higher until it became too much. The tension coiled tighter, tighter still until she felt as though she might snap.

"Come for us, Lindy," Hayden growled in her ear, nipping her shoulder.

Her body exploded, white spots dancing across her vision, a tsunami crashing through her insides as her orgasm ripped her to shreds. She hadn't thought it possible.

"Fuck…" Micah roared. "Ahh, God… Yes!"

Hayden's body slammed into hers once more, and she felt him pulse inside her as he, too, came.

Lindy tried to stay lucid, tried to fight the blackness that was dragging her under, but when Micah pulled her to him, his warm arms banding around her, she knew she would lose the battle.

"We've got you, sweet girl."

Those were the last words she heard before she succumbed to the overwhelming exhaustion.

19

Two weeks later...

"Have you heard from Lindy?" Hayden asked when he joined Micah in the hotel coffee shop.

"I did," he told him.

Hayden cocked his head, glaring at him.

Micah fought the urge to laugh.

"What did she say?"

"She said she'd be ready at seven."

Hayden nodded.

For the past two weeks, ever since they'd taken Lindy back to her apartment after the incredible night they'd spent together, Micah had been working to seduce her the right way. With Hayden's help, of course.

Micah didn't try to hide the fact that he wanted her with a passion he could hardly contain. He had talked to her every single day since, enjoying getting to know her on an entirely different level. The three of them had gone out to dinner, to the club, even caught a show one night. They didn't see her nearly as much as Micah would like, though. Micah knew that Hayden was talking to her, as well, during the days they didn't get to spend time in her presence. It was like rapid dating, although they'd started with sex in the beginning and had yet to follow through again. Not because the connection wasn't there. It was and it was rather intense, but again, Micah was trying to prove a point.

Between her nine-to-five job and their ridiculous hours, it wasn't that easy to sync their schedules, but they'd managed to make it happen tonight, and Micah was looking forward to spending the entire night with both of them again.

When the barista passed over two cups of coffee, Micah thanked her, then handed one to Hayden. They found an empty spot in the far corner and sat down.

"What's on your mind?" Hayden asked, obviously picking up on his mood.

Micah shook his head, not wanting to voice his insecurities. He knew they were stupid, yet he'd allowed them to plague him for the past two weeks.

In his thirty-eight years, he'd never fallen in love with anyone.

Until Hayden.

Yes, he could admit to himself that Hayden had enthralled him, pulled him right into his orbit. Micah loved him.

He wasn't quite there with Lindy, but he was quickly working his way in that direction, despite the fact that they'd known each other for such a short time. Time meant nothing to him in the grand scheme of things. He knew you couldn't measure emotion based on seconds, so that wasn't the part that bothered him.

"Talk to me," Hayden urged, leaning in closer, his eyes locked with Micah's.

Keeping his voice low, he gave in. "Does this seem too good to be true?"

"What? Lindy?"

Micah shook his head. "Us. You and me. And Lindy."

"There's an us?" Hayden looked genuinely surprised.

"Why wouldn't there be?"

Hayden shrugged, then seemed engrossed in the steam coming out of his cup.

"Look at me," Micah insisted.

He waited until his lover turned toward him. "Do you not want this?"

"Of course I do," he snapped. "I've wanted it for a long damn time."

"Then what's the problem?" Micah wasn't sure how this had turned into an issue, but he felt the tension between them.

"She's going to take this slow," Hayden admitted. "That's the way she works."

"Then we'll take it slow."

Hayden's gaze lowered once again. "I don't want us to take it slow because she does."

"Have we slowed down?" Micah had never really defined what was going on between them.

"We haven't spent the night together since she left."

Micah did a quick trip through the memories of the past two weeks and realized Hayden was right. How the hell had that happened?

"We've both been wrapped up in her," Hayden offered. "To the point we've neglected ... us."

Micah nodded because he couldn't refute that. He wasn't sure how it had happened, but Hayden was right.

He glanced at his watch. "I need to shower. Meet me in my room at six thirty?"

Hayden's eyes widened, but he nodded.

Yeah, Micah knew he'd cut that conversation off, but he had a good reason.

A very good reason.

He waited until Hayden headed back downstairs before he grabbed his phone and dialed Lindy's number.

"Hey." Her voice was so soft, so sweet.

He missed her.

"Change of plans."

"Oh, yeah?" She sounded intrigued. He'd hoped she would be.

"Yeah. Can you come to me tonight?"

"Is that some sort of innuendo?"

Micah chuckled. "I didn't mean it that way, but I'm definitely going to make you come tonight."

"I'm not sure what you and Hayden have done to me, Micah Fontenot…"

"Not enough, sweet girl, I assure you," he said with a grin. "Can you be here at six? At the hotel? I've got something in mind for Hayden."

"Something dirty?"

"Absolutely." He started down the hallway toward the offices. "I need to prove to him how much he means to me."

"Oh... Is there something wrong?"

"No, sweet girl. Everything's right. I'm just feeling my way through this, just like you and Hayden are."

"This is a little different, huh?"

"By different, you mean crazy good?"

"Of course." Lindy's laughter rippled through the phone.

God, he loved that sound.

"I'll see you at six?"

"I'll be there."

20

Hayden made it to Micah's room by six forty-five, rather than six thirty as promised. He'd had to juggle his timeline when he found out that Max Adorite, the owner of Devil's Playground, was in town. It meant Hayden had to provide security for the man and get him to where he needed to be.

He probably should've called Micah to let him know, but after their conversation over coffee, Hayden felt like an asshole. For one, he shouldn't have made a big deal about this thing that was going on between them. He wasn't jealous of Lindy. Quite the opposite, actually. He liked where this was going, but he happened to like what he and Micah had originally as well. In his opinion, Lindy was the icing on the cake. Micah was quite clear as to how he felt about her, and Hayden was open about his feelings for her as well. And he felt like a selfish bastard for having brought it up.

Not that he could change any of that now.

He knocked on the door, expecting Micah to be waiting so they could head downstairs.

When the door opened, Micah wasn't the one standing there.

Hayden tried to keep his jaw from coming unhinged when he saw Lindy wearing an indecently short silk robe and a pair of red do-me heels. He allowed his gaze to slowly trail up the length of her phenomenal legs, higher to the plump swell of her breasts barely hidden by the silk, then up to her face.

Her smile flashed as she took a step back and opened the door.

Clearly he'd missed a memo or something.

Stepping inside, Hayden waited for her to close the door.

"Hi," she greeted, moving up close to him and pressing her lips to his.

She smelled fantastic.

"I missed you," she whispered, her tone soft and sweet, an erotic seduction.

"I missed you, too." Wrapping his arms around her, Hayden took full advantage of the moment, kissing her with all the pent-up frustration coursing through him. Ever since the night they'd spent together, he'd been counting down the minutes until he could get his hands on her again.

"Micah's waiting for you," she mumbled against his mouth. "And I promise, you're not gonna want to keep him waiting."

Hayden reluctantly released her, noting the teasing tone.

"For me? Why is he waiting for me?"

Lindy took his hand and tugged him farther into the room. "Don't ask questions."

Micah was standing in the living room, staring out the window overlooking the Strip. It wasn't quite dark yet, but night was approaching quickly.

"Sit," Micah instructed.

Part of him wanted to defy the instruction, but there was a hint of dominance in Micah's voice that appealed to him on so many levels. It was one of the things he truly loved about the man.

Lindy took the chair, which left the small sofa. Unbuttoning his jacket, Hayden slowly took a seat, glancing between the two of them.

Micah walked around behind Lindy, his big hands trailing over her shoulders, then sliding down between her breasts, intimately caressing her. Hayden's dick went rock hard instantly.

"You mentioned you like to watch," Lindy said, her voice husky.

"I do," he admitted, his eyes darting between the two of them.

"Turns out, I do, too."

Okay. He wasn't sure what to say to that.

"I was thinking about something you said today," Micah began, his hands still sliding over Lindy. "And you're right. I have neglected you lately. Not on purpose, mind you. This is new for me. For us. This might be my ultimate fantasy, having both of you in my bed ... always ... so it's going to take me some time to adapt."

Hayden understood that.

"But I'm willing to make it up to you."

Leaning back, Hayden casually crossed his ankle over his knee, staring at Micah, urging him to continue.

116

"Tonight's about you and me."

Hayden cocked an eyebrow. He liked where this was going. Especially since Lindy was evidently in agreement. It meant she would ultimately be with them. Watching.

And wasn't that an incredibly scorching thought.

"She's not allowed to touch," Micah noted, his hands dipping deeper into her robe, separating the two parts, baring her breasts to Hayden as Micah cupped them.

"But you can," she noted. "I'm content to watch the two of you." She fanned herself, still smiling. "And you're welcome to do whatever you want to me."

"Fuck me," Hayden mumbled under his breath. This was obviously some sort of role play the two of them had concocted, and fuck if it didn't make him harder than he'd ever been.

"There's only one catch," Micah added.

That was definitely more Micah's style. "Which would be…?"

"You only do what I tell you to do."

"Okay." Hayden didn't mind taking orders from Micah. He enjoyed it, actually.

"And I get to do to you whatever I want."

Now, Hayden could definitely live with that.

21

When Micah had asked her to come to his place, Lindy didn't hesitate to agree. Once she got here, she'd been surprised to find out he'd asked her to arrive earlier than Hayden. And when he'd laid out his plan for the man, Lindy was almost positive she fell a little more in love with him.

Yes, she'd said it. She was in love.

Okay, it probably wasn't practical, but she couldn't deny it. She was in love with both men. Yep. Two men. These past couple of weeks had been unbelievable. She'd spent every waking moment of every day thinking about them both. About the night they'd shared together, about the little conversations they'd had since they'd taken her back to her apartment. She was so preoccupied she could hardly focus on work.

And now this…

Lindy had known from the beginning that Micah and Hayden had been a thing before she'd come into the picture. They'd openly admitted it. And when Micah had informed her that he'd unintentionally neglected Hayden these past two weeks, she'd felt his pain. Although he was setting this seduction up, she knew Micah wasn't simply denoting sex when he referred to neglect. He cared about Hayden deeply.

Some would probably think she should be jealous, but she wasn't. The fact that she was here for this was proof that they wanted her here. Did she have her own insecurities? Absolutely. Did she know where this was headed? No. But she fully intended to ride it out with them. It might take some time, because they were all three new to this, but she liked it that way. And the fact that Micah openly admitted he'd handled it badly but was willing to make up for it had sealed the deal for her.

"Stand up," Micah instructed Hayden.

Lindy's body was already humming from Micah's ministrations earlier. The way he touched her made every nerve ending flare to life. She wanted one of them to touch her, but she understood this was Micah's show. She would sit back and watch. And she would like it.

Hayden slowly got to his feet, his eyes never leaving Micah's face. Lindy could see the anticipation in his expression, in the way he held himself completely still. Micah obviously knew what Hayden liked, and he was giving the man what he wanted.

For the next five minutes—maybe ten—Lindy watched in awe as Micah slowly undressed Hayden. Lord have mercy, it was like unwrapping the best Christmas present ever. No, it was like watching the best Christmas present ever being unwrapped by a super-hot guy.

What was interesting was how Micah kept his touch light, moving around Hayden, his fingers gliding over smooth, golden skin and taut, rippling muscle. She was mesmerized, completely enraptured by both of them.

"So fucking hot," Micah breathed against Hayden's neck, leaning in to kiss him gently.

Hayden's erection bobbed urgently, as though begging for attention. However, Micah didn't give in to him. He simply continued to fondle and tease with the tips of his fingers and the slightest brush of his lips.

Lindy could see Hayden's pulse throbbing in his neck. The man was hanging by a thread.

Micah urged Hayden toward the window, placing Hayden's palms flat on the glass a little above his head. Lindy admired Hayden's exquisite form, the way his butt muscles flexed, his shoulders tensed.

"Too bad the whole strip can't see you right now," Micah told him, walking around behind him. "You'd like that, wouldn't you?"

"Yeah," Hayden said on a rush of air.

"Would you like them to see me sucking your cock?"

"Fuck yes."

Micah slipped between Hayden and the window, lowering himself to his knees. The man was still fully dressed, wearing what was probably a three-thousand-dollar suit. It didn't seem to faze him.

"Remember, no touching," Micah reminded, planting his hands flat on Hayden's thighs. "And you can't come."

Lindy couldn't tear her eyes off the sight of the two men together. From her spot in the chair, she could see Micah fully, watching as Hayden's cock slipped past his lips. Micah didn't use his hands, sucking him slowly, deeply. She could see Hayden's muscles tense the longer Micah tormented him.

It felt like hours but was probably only minutes. Nonetheless, the more Micah teased Hayden, the hornier she became. Lindy hadn't been sure how she'd feel about this game once they got started, but so far so good.

Hayden growled, an obvious attempt to hold back. Lindy watched as Micah released Hayden's cock, then stared up at him.

He seemed to contemplate something for a moment before getting to his feet.

"Stay right where you are."

Hayden didn't move, didn't even turn. Micah came to stand behind her, his hands once again gliding over her chest, inching lower until he was pinching her nipples.

"You like what you see so far?"

"Of course." How could she not?

Although his breath fanned her cheek, Micah's voice wasn't soft when he added, "I want to see his mouth on your pussy. Would you like that?"

"Oh, yes."

"Good girl."

For whatever reason, with those two words whispered from Micah's mouth … she was willing and ready to do his bidding. Apparently Hayden was intimately familiar with this side of Micah.

Just when she thought it couldn't get any hotter.

22

Micah took his time getting undressed, keeping an eye on Hayden and Lindy while he did. He didn't think he would ever get enough of these two. Ever.

He already knew that they would be pursuing this further, seeing what would come of this relationship. How it would turn out would be anyone's guess, but if they kept on at this pace, they'd be taking things to the next level in the very near future.

Micah already hoped that was the case. He didn't want to spend too much time trying to figure out the when, where, and how. He wasn't getting any younger, that was for damn sure.

"Come here, sweet girl," Micah demanded, holding out his hand for Lindy.

She got up from the chair, taking his hand.

"Come here, love," he ordered Hayden.

The man dropped his hands from the window and paced across the floor to where Micah was now sitting with Lindy on the sofa. He positioned her so that she was on his lap, her back to his chest, her legs spread wide, his cock nestled against her ass.

"On your knees."

Hayden went to his knees before them.

"Sweet girl, move your panties out of the way."

Lindy tugged her panties to the side, revealing her smooth, hairless pussy. God, he loved that she was completely bare. It gave him an unobstructed view of her delicate pink flesh.

"Spread her with your fingers," Micah instructed.

Hayden did, his eyes never moving from her slick folds.

"Don't move your hands from where they are," Micah told Hayden. "Now make her come."

Lindy sucked in a deep breath when Hayden's mouth descended on her cunt. Micah reached around and clamped his fingers on her nipples. "And you … don't move either."

She groaned, but he didn't think she was disappointed in his instruction.

"You like his tongue on your pussy? The way he licks your clit?"

"Mmm-hmm."

Micah shifted her so he could get a better view, loving how Hayden didn't hesitate, licking and sucking her, making Lindy moan and gasp as he used nothing more than his lips and tongue to drive her to ecstasy.

"Make her come," Micah insisted. "And when you do, I'm going to fuck your ass and make you beg me to let you come."

Hayden moaned, his eyes darting up to Micah's. Micah could see the dare in his eyes. Hayden always did like when Micah took complete control. That was a good thing considering he liked being in control. At all times.

Although, he'd be the first to admit, these two could make him lose it relatively quickly.

Adjusting Lindy again, Micah pulled her higher on him so he could get his dick near Hayden's mouth.

"Suck me, then lick her."

Hayden kept his fingers right where Micah told him to, his mouth lowering over his shaft, sucking him hard and deep, just the way Micah liked it. Hayden alternated between licking Lindy's pussy, pushing her closer to the edge, then back to Micah. He was drawing it out, that was clear. If it weren't for the look of sheer pleasure on Hayden's face, Micah would've pushed him to take her over the edge.

"Don't make me come," Micah warned, pulling his hips back and forcing his dick from Hayden's exquisite mouth.

Without question, Hayden dove back down on Lindy, working her with his tongue, his full attention on her clit. She writhed and moaned on Micah's lap, but she didn't move her hands, didn't try to take control.

"Oh … God… Don't stop…" Her words were barely a whisper. "Please don't stop. Right there … right there…" Her cry of release echoed in the room, making Micah's cock jerk wildly. He could so easily slip inside her, fuck her to another orgasm, but he refrained. He wanted Hayden with an intensity that wasn't foreign to him. It'd always been that way with Hayden.

Micah settled Lindy on the couch beside him, kissing her lips softly before getting up and pulling Hayden up with him. He had Hayden resume his position at the window, overlooking Sin City while he sheathed himself with a condom and lubed his cock.

Kissing Hayden's neck, Micah pushed two fingers into his ass. "Do you know how bad I want to be inside you right now?"

Hayden didn't respond, but he tilted his head, offering Micah access to his neck.

"I fucking dream of this," he admitted, his voice low but not low enough that Lindy wouldn't hear. He wasn't keeping anything from her, but he was going to tell Hayden how he felt.

"I dream about waking up with you in my bed, going to sleep after you fuck me into oblivion. That's where I want you, Hay. I want you there every goddamn night."

Pulling his fingers from Hayden's ass, Micah replaced them with his cock, pushing in deep as he forced Hayden to bend over slightly. Micah covered him with his body, twining his fingers with Hayden's against the glass as he rocked his hips, pushing in deep, withdrawing only slightly. He continued to fuck him just like that, never fully retreating from his body.

"Do you want that, too? Do you want to be in my bed every night? You and Lindy? Wake up to us each morning? Let us love you every night?"

"It's what I want," Hayden confirmed, grunting as Micah penetrated him deeper.

Micah kissed Hayden's neck, then turned to look at Lindy. She was still watching them, her eyes glazed over. "Come over here, baby."

She got to her feet and sauntered over, looking like a wet fucking dream.

"Suck him," he whispered, leaning over and kissing her softly. "While I fuck him."

He could see the heat glimmering in her pale blue eyes. She instantly went to her knees in front of Hayden, but Micah could no longer see her.

But Hayden's hiss said it all.

23

Hayden's heart was pounding like a bass drum. He could feel it slamming against his ribs. Or he had been able to, rather, right up until Lindy took his cock to the back of her throat, humming softly, sending vibrations shooting straight to his balls.

He was quickly losing it. With Micah leaning over him, his hands pressing Hayden's against the glass, he couldn't move, couldn't do anything more than endure the hard shaft in his ass, the sweet lips around his dick, doing nothing more than teasing him.

"This is what we'll give you," Micah whispered. "I'll claim you every damn night if I have to. Prove to you that you belong to me, to us."

Hayden felt himself crumbling. Micah wasn't known for sharing his feelings, and though he had his own way of going about it, Hayden knew this was it. This was Micah's way of telling him that he loved him, even if he never shared those three words with him. In truth, Hayden didn't need to hear them, but he did need this. The warmth of Micah against him, holding him together, Lindy right there with them.

Yeah, this was new for them, but it was definitely what Hayden wanted. He knew that rushing Lindy wasn't going to be an option. She was a strong-willed woman, keen to explore her sexual side, but getting to her heart was going to be another story. He wouldn't lie, he wanted her to love them, to welcome them into her life with open arms. He wanted it more than his next breath, but he was scared if they pushed too hard, they would scare her off. Hayden knew they would eventually get there, eventually make her fall in love with them, but in the meantime, he would have to learn how to enjoy the ride.

Micah's hips began moving faster, while Lindy allowed the momentum to guide Hayden's cock deeper into her mouth.

"I love you," Micah whispered against his ear. "Fucking love you. Every goddamn thing about you. More than that, I need you. In my life. In my bed."

Hayden didn't have any warning; he came in a rush as the words penetrated. Lindy swallowed him down, then slipped away while Micah began fucking him in earnest, driving deeper until he came, fingers still locked with Hayden's.

The next thing Hayden knew, Micah had pulled Lindy up beside them, holding her while Micah remained buried deep inside his ass.

"Did I prove my point?" Micah asked, his words soft, gentle.

"Yeah."

When Micah pulled out, he spun Hayden around to face them, their mouths fusing together, tongues tangling. They alternated; Hayden kissed Lindy with equal passion, wanting her to know that the feelings went three ways. The emotions that had been at war a moment ago settled, no longer in chaos.

For the first time in his life, Hayden knew what he wanted.

Better than that, he knew that he had it.

Right here.

With both of them.

24

Lindy woke up to find herself in Micah's bed. Only there was no Micah. She felt behind her to see if Hayden was there. Nope. His side was empty as well.

She rolled to her back, thinking back on last night, on all that had happened. After Micah proved his point to Hayden, they had both focused all of their attention on her. For a few minutes, Lindy had actually had to battle the green-eyed monster. Seeing the two men together, pleasuring one another didn't bother her in the least. She enjoyed it immensely, far more than she ever thought was possible.

But when Micah admitted to Hayden that he loved him, she'd been a little jealous.

Then again, she'd only known them for two weeks. They'd been together for months. It only made sense.

And yes, she was fighting to keep her rational side on the forefront. She wasn't prone to giving in to emotion or letting it lead her around by the nose. Falling in love wasn't something she'd envisioned for herself. She was a realist and she'd thought for sure love would simply pass her by.

Until Hayden and Micah had come into her world.

Everything had changed at that point.

Oddly enough, she wasn't upset, but she wanted a little more. The fact was, Lindy knew it was her fault. Over the past couple of weeks, she had continued to reiterate that she wanted to take this slow. More to protect her heart than anything else.

She heard the rustle of carpet when the door pushed open. There was no way she could pretend she was asleep, so she pasted on a smile and glanced up to see Hayden standing there. He was wearing a pair of jeans and nothing else. She briefly wondered if he kept jeans here or if he'd gone to his room at some point last night.

"Morning, sleepyhead." Hayden tapped the door shut behind him and joined her on the bed, lying down beside her.

"How long have you been up?" she inquired.

"Micah had to take care of something at the club several hours ago, so I got up when he did."

NICOLE EDWARDS

"Oh." Which meant she'd slept most of the night alone.

Hayden's head tilted. "What's wrong?"

"Nothing... I ... uh..." She looked around for her clothes, then remembered they were in the bathroom, where she'd changed before Hayden had arrived. "I should probably get going. I didn't mean to—"

Hayden shut her up with a kiss that melted her instantly. She quickly sank into his arms, savoring the taste of him. The kiss went a long way to easing the chaos that had been in her heart moments ago.

"I was waiting until you woke up to take a shower. Care to join me?"

"What about Micah?"

His eyebrows shot down. "Do you need him here?"

"No ... I just..." Lindy dropped her head back on the pillow. "Can I be honest?"

"I'd hope you would be."

"I'm so confused about what's going on here. How I'm supposed to act, if I'm supposed to only be involved when the two of you are together. I don't know how this works. Until that first night..."

Hayden waited for her, but Lindy didn't know what she was trying to say. Thankfully, he climbed out of bed and tugged her along behind him. She followed him into the bathroom, waited while he turned on the shower and discarded his jeans. And when the warm water was cascading over her, his even warmer body practically wrapped around her, Lindy relaxed.

"This works however we want it to," Hayden explained, his voice soft. "We both want you. We both want each other. And we hope you want both of us."

"I do."

"Then that's the only rule. If we keep this within those parameters, I don't know how we could go wrong."

Hayden reached over and grabbed something off the ledge.

Before she could process what he was doing, Hayden had rolled a condom over his erection and backed her up against the tiled wall.

"I want you, Lindy. I woke up this morning wanting to slide inside you and remain there for the entire day."

She didn't get a chance for a rebuttal because he kissed her thoroughly, his tongue sliding against hers, his hands warm and firm against her skin.

"Let me love you, Lindy. You simply have to let me in. I can tell you right now, Micah and I are waiting for you. We both know what we want from you, how we feel about you. We won't rush you, but we won't let you go, either."

His words were melting her heart, turning her to mush.

When he lifted her leg up against his hip, Lindy sighed into his mouth.

"Are you ready for me?"

Lindy nodded. She was more than ready.

When he pushed inside her, his cock filling her completely, she nearly came undone. She'd spent the past two weeks trying to divide her time between the two of them, wanting to give them both what they wanted from her. It wasn't easy to do, but right now, it was only her and Hayden, and she let herself love him back while he made love to her right there in Micah's shower.

His hands slid up, cupping her breasts, lifting them as he leaned down and tongued her nipples. He never stopped pumping his hips, fucking her sweetly, gently. She was unraveling faster than she'd thought possible.

"Let go, Lindy. You don't have to hold back for me."

She did. Lindy allowed her orgasm to take her, rolling through her body in sweet rapture. It wasn't the intense orgasm Hayden and Micah had given her before, but it was memorable.

"God, you're beautiful."

Lindy opened her eyes to see Hayden watching her, his expression reflecting the same love and adoration she'd seen when he looked at Micah. It filled her with longing, with hope. Wrapping her arms around him, she pulled him closer, kissing him while he continued to thrust into her over and over again. She didn't stop until he groaned, his body stilling, his cock pulsing inside her.

She knew, at this point, there was no stopping her free fall. It was inevitable.

Lindy could only hope that they were both there to catch her.

25

When Micah returned to his suite to find Lindy and Hayden in the shower together, he hadn't wanted to interrupt. That didn't stop him from watching, listening. He couldn't resist. Watching them together might possibly be his new favorite pastime. Hayden was so gentle with her, knowing exactly what Lindy needed.

Micah knew how that worked, because Hayden was the same way with him.

The shower water shut off, and when the glass door opened, Lindy's eyes widened.

"Micah…"

He smiled. Grabbing a towel, he remained where he was, leaning against the vanity. "Come here, sweet girl."

She walked right over to him, water dripping down her beautiful body. He wrapped her in the towel, wiping her face, her shoulders, all while admiring her.

139

"How long have you been there?"

"Long enough." Long enough to know that Hayden was right, they would give her all the time she needed, but they weren't letting her go.

"Did you enjoy the show?" Hayden joked, clearly trying to assure Lindy that this was okay.

"More than you know." He locked his eyes with Lindy's. "I love watching the two of you together."

"I should probably get dressed," Lindy said, gripping the towel to her chest.

"Why?" Micah leaned down and brushed her lips with his. "We'll just have to remove it later."

She smiled, and this time it didn't look forced.

"Why don't I order room service and we crawl back in bed for a couple of hours. It's Sunday, so we've got all day."

Lindy nodded. "I'd like that."

Micah cupped her face and kissed her, pushing his tongue into her mouth. "And if you're lucky, I might let you go to work tomorrow."

"If I'm lucky, huh?"

He nodded, sliding his thumb over her plump lower lip. He scanned her eyes to see if she was hiding anything. He'd heard what Hayden told her in the shower.

"On the other hand, why don't we skip breakfast so we can spend the rest of the morning loving you."

Her eyes lowered and the color in her cheeks rose. When she looked up at him, he saw so much emotion there.

"Only the morning?" she asked, her tone tentative.

Hayden moved in, sandwiching her between them.

"All day," Micah whispered. "Or for the rest of our lives. It's up to you, sweet girl. This is right where we want to be. How fast or how slow we move is now up to you."

As far as Micah was concerned, he had everything he needed right here.

Everything.

Epilogue

Two months later

"She's going to need more space than this," Hayden insisted, watching as Micah opened drawer after drawer, all of them full.

"Which is why we're buying the condo," Micah replied, peering up at Hayden as though that said it all.

Hayden held up the floor plan he was referring to. "Exactly what I'm talking about."

Micah closed the last drawer and moved closer. "So, you're saying we go with the three-bedroom?"

"Yes," he confirmed. "She'll have her own office, plus there's a guest bedroom."

Micah's eyebrow quirked. "As long as y'all understand no one gets their own room. We're all sleeping together."

Hayden chuckled. "I don't think anyone has asked for anything other than that."

It was true. The three of them were still working through this new relationship, although they'd made tremendous strides in recent weeks. They spent a lot of time together, during the week and on the weekend. Whenever they weren't working, the three of them were usually together here in Micah's suite. However, they'd learned that they needed more space than this afforded them. At least in the long term. It was enough for them to sleep in, but in order for them to be comfortable, they needed to have room to spread out.

"Is the closet big enough?" Micah questioned, tapping his finger on the piece of paper in Hayden's hand.

"If not, we'll have someone build a bigger one," Hayden told him, desperately wanting someone to make a final decision so they could put an offer in and get the ball rolling.

"I want this done yesterday," Micah grumbled. "I don't want any more excuses. I want her in my bed with us every single night."

"She wants that, too."

Hayden turned at the sound of Lindy's voice coming from behind him. He smiled to himself.

"So, the three-bedroom then?" Micah asked, glancing over to Lindy, then back to Hayden.

It was hard to fight the urge to sigh in frustration. Lindy was the only one concerned about the three-bedroom condo. She was insistent that it was more money than they needed to spend and that two bedrooms would work just fine. Hayden didn't want to tell her that money wasn't an issue.

When Lindy didn't answer, Micah reached for her, pulling her into him. Hayden placed the sheet of paper on the dresser and moved to stand behind her.

"Say yes," Micah urged.

"Or we'll strip you naked and fuck you within an inch of your life until you do," Hayden whispered teasingly.

"That's a threat?" Lindy laughed, a beautiful sound that made Hayden's heart swell. God, he loved this woman.

"She's got a point," Micah joked. "She's insatiable as it is. Practically a nymphomaniac. Probably get more out of her if you threaten to withhold sex."

Lindy giggled, trying to move out from between them. Hayden grabbed her hips to still her.

"I'm not the insatiable one, Micah Fontenot," she countered, still laughing.

"Make the decision," Hayden insisted, sliding his hands up beneath her shirt. "Or the nakedness will commence."

Lindy moaned when Hayden cupped her breasts, squeezing gently, teasing her nipples through the thin lace of her bra.

"Yes," she moaned. "Yes to three bedrooms if it'll shut you up. And yes to you continuing to do ... that."

Micah leaned down, his lips brushing Lindy's while Hayden watched them, his hands still groping her.

"Strip her," Micah demanded, smiling at Hayden over Lindy's shoulder. "It's time to consummate this deal."

Again Lindy struggled to pull away, laughing as she did. Hayden loved the sound, loved to see so much happiness shining in her eyes. They had agreed to make this permanent, to move in together, to live happily ever after, and Hayden knew Micah wasn't the only antsy one. Hayden was tired of sleeping without her, too.

"I think a hand shake will suffice," Lindy mused.

Hayden reached for her hands, lowering one so that it covered the bulge in Micah's slacks, the other on his own erection. "How about we use your hands for other things?"

"You boys are ridiculous," she moaned again when Micah's head lowered so that his mouth engulfed her breast.

"But you love us," Hayden stated, pushing his cock against her hand.

"True, I do love you. Both of you." She smiled at Hayden over her shoulder. "Even if I never seem to get my way."

"I'll give it to you any which way you like," Micah said, going to his knees before her.

Hayden knew exactly where this was headed.

"Not what I meant," she countered with a long sigh. "But I'll take it."

"Of course you will," Hayden whispered softly. "And you'll like it."

"True."

Micah managed to shove her jeans down her legs while Hayden stripped her shirt from her body.

"Now quit squirming," Micah insisted, smiling up at them. "And let us love you."

"For the rest of the afternoon," Hayden added.

"How about for the rest of my life?" Lindy said.

"Okay, deal," Hayden and Micah said at the exact same time.

Keep reading for an excerpt from

Beautifully Brutal
Southern Boy Mafia, 1

Acknowledgments

I have to thank my family first, for putting up with my craziness. From my sudden outbursts when I think of something that needs to be added or when I question why one of the characters did what they did, to the strange hours that I keep and the days on end when I'm MIA because I'm under deadline or just engrossed in a story... Y'all are incredibly tolerant of me and for that, I am forever grateful. I love you with all that I am.

My street team – The Naughty & Nice Girls. Ladies, your daily pimping and support fills my heart with so much love. You are a blessing to me, each and every one of you.

My beta readers, Chancy and Amber. Ladies, I'm not sure thanks will ever be enough. However, not only are you the ones who catch the weird things and ask the bigger questions, you've both become my friends and you keep me going.

My copyeditor, Amy. Punctuation and grammar... well, that's not my strong suit. But it is yours and you are truly remarkable at what you do. You simply amaze me and I am so glad that I found you.

Nicole Nation 2.0 for the constant support and love. This group of ladies has kept me going for so long, I'm not sure I'd know what to do without them.

And, of course, YOU, the reader. Your emails, messages, posts, comments, tweets… they mean more to me than you can imagine. I thrive on hearing from you, knowing that my characters and my stories have touched you in some way keeps me going. I've been known to shed a tear or two when reading an email because you simply bring so much joy to my life with your support. I thank you for that.

♥••••♥••••♥

About Nicole

New York Times and *USA Today* bestselling author Nicole Edwards lives in Austin, Texas with her husband, their three kids, and four rambunctious dogs. When she's not writing about sexy alpha males, Nicole can often be found with her Kindle in hand or making an attempt to keep the dogs happy. You can find her hanging out on Facebook and interacting with her readers - even when she's supposed to be writing.

Nicole also writes contemporary/new adult romance as Timberlyn Scott.

Website
www.NicoleEdwardsAuthor.com

Facebook
www.facebook.com/Author.Nicole.Edwards

Twitter
@NicoleEAuthor

Chapter One

It starts the same as it ends.
Beautifully brutal.

Twenty-four months ago

Maximillian Adorite studied the woman strolling toward him, curious as to why she had graced him with her presence tonight of all nights.

Coincidence?

No. Couldn't be.

Max didn't believe in coincidence.

Despite his interest in who she was and why she was there, on the very night when a potential shit storm was brewing around him, he found himself transfixed by her, something that didn't usually happen to him.

Not like this.

In his world, women were a dime a dozen. He credited that to the wealth and danger that surrounded him. Women liked bad boys, and Max's reputation definitely qualified him for that list. Then again, the women he shared his time with usually figured that out the morning after, when he—politely, if he had been interested enough to catch her name—asked them to leave.

However, this dark-haired beauty ... the one with the most striking eyes he'd ever seen—they literally glowed white—was so intriguing he'd found himself watching her for most of the night. But that was all he'd done. Because this woman wasn't the type who would warm his sheets for only a few hours. He knew that instantly, and since he wasn't interested in anything more than a couple of hours, he had fought the urge to introduce himself.

Then again, she knew who he was. He was the very reason she was there, or so he'd been told. It'd been his idea to offer the invitation so he could get more information on her, see her in action. This woman ... she was his enemy, and Max was interested in keeping her close, getting to know more about her to determine if she was the threat he'd been told she was.

Not that he was all too worried about what she did or didn't want from him. Or vice versa.

He could sense by her nearness that she was a distraction he definitely didn't need. Especially tonight. Seeing as he was the host of this party—or what appeared to be a party from the outside looking in and was, in fact, the announcement of a transfer of power—she was a temptation he should avoid but one he couldn't bring himself to stray too far from. And here she was, successfully keeping him from his other guests, yet he couldn't muster an ounce of regret.

"And you are?" he asked innocuously, holding his hand out to greet her when she approached.

"*Courtney Kogan,*" she replied firmly, a hint of defiance in her raspy tone, in the subtle way she tilted her chin as she spoke. "*But I suppose you already knew that.*"

A battle of wills.

Very intriguing.

With his hand still hovering between them, he waited for her to slide her fingers against his palm. Never taking his eyes off her face, his gaze locked with hers, Max allowed his brain to process her touch, his body hardening instantly. Bringing her fingers to his lips, he kissed her knuckles softly, inhaling the subtle yet sexy scent of her perfume, something warm and exotic—much like her—with a hint of jasmine and amber wood drifting toward him. Intoxicating.

"*Nice to meet you, Courtney Kogan.*"

Max hadn't needed the formal introduction, however; he still would've recognized the name, known who she was, who she worked for, and why she was there, but he kept his expression masked.

"*Don't be so sure of that,*" she said, a throaty drawl accompanying her words while her satisfied grin hinted at something darker, far more dangerous than what he'd expected from her. From a distance, Courtney had appeared sweet, perhaps a little shy even, but up close, she was anything but.

There was a glimmer of determination in her white-gray eyes, the kohl liner making her look slightly intimidating and a little older than the twenty-four years he knew her to be. The daring smirk on her glossy lips and a hint of a blush on her high, delicate cheekbones contradicted that steely resolve, though.

No, this woman wasn't sweet or shy. She was a contradiction. A dangerous one if he had to guess.

Max knew all about dark and dangerous. It was his life. He was the son of Samuel and Genevieve Adorite, and Max's world was entrenched in the dark and dirty underworld that his parents had proudly built around them.

Southern Boy Mafia, they called them.

Max wasn't one to put labels on himself or his family, but he couldn't deny the fact that, by definition, that was exactly what they were. Mafia.

No, there weren't any Italian roots in his family, nor were they tied to any of the five families directly, didn't have any involvement with the Cosa Nostra, either, but they were, in fact, connected. Even without those direct ties, they were extremely powerful, more so than most people realized, which had brought them to the attention of some of the most formidable families in the world.

His father, Samuel, was the leader of the Adorite family—known to all as the boss. Before him had been Max's grandfather, Floyd, and before him, Max's great-grandfather, Andrew. And so on and so forth. Throughout time, control of their extremely profitable businesses had remained within the family, transferring to the eldest male child, although their organization, spanning the vast state of Texas, was made up of much more than that.

Max had recently moved into the position of underboss, a rank within the hierarchy that had been set out for him from the beginning. At least until he would take over the entire organization from his father. Until recently, the second-in-command position had been held by Samuel's younger brother, Nick. However, since Nick's stroke three months ago, which had resulted in Max's uncle being partially paralyzed and suffering from immense neurological damage leaving him unable to make decisions critical to his position, Max had taken over. As had always been the intention.

At twenty-seven, Max was now the second most powerful man in their organization. Despite the number, Max certainly didn't feel young. In fact, he felt decades older, thanks to the toll this world had taken on him.

Not that he spent his days worried about his next birthday or the chain of command or that the media had dubbed them the Southern Boy Mafia sometime in the late sixties. Business was business, and it just so happened that their family dabbled in plenty of money-making opportunities.

Were they legal? Some of them, sure. Others, no. But that was the way of the world.

Max's respect for his father and the family ran far and wide, and he'd been born into a life that would forever be based on a strict structure, so Max had fallen into the position as was expected of him, which he took very seriously.

As for his three brothers, Brent, Victor, and Aidan, as well as his two sisters, Ashlynn and Madison, they were all involved in the family business in one way or another, or, as in Victor's and Madison's case, they were finishing school before they devoted themselves fully. Both of Max's youngest siblings were currently in law school. Although the rest of them had all handled their own aspect of the organization as they'd seen fit since the day they'd each turned twenty-one, they still reported directly to Max, always had, even before this change. Not that he was certain what they were doing most of the time, but he made a valiant effort to keep up with them when he could.

The one thing he knew with utmost certainty was that people feared him, feared what his family was capable of. And rightfully so. With the help of his right-hand man, Leyton Matheson, Max fully intended to carry on the business, as well as the family name.

But right here, right now, with this woman in the sparkling silver gown that accentuated her perfect curves—the kind of curves a man could easily grab hold of—he wasn't worried about business or family, or even money, for that matter.

He was curious as to what her game was.

"And why do you say that?" he probed, amused and intrigued in equal measure.

"No reason," she stated off-handedly, her gaze sliding down to his mouth briefly before breaking away completely. "I should let you get back to your guests. I merely wanted to thank you for inviting me."

Max nodded, once again studying her. She was an enigma. Her body language was saying things her luscious lips weren't, but he could tell with this particular woman, her brain called all the shots. If he had to guess, she didn't listen much to what her body wanted. Something else that fascinated him where she was concerned.

"I look forward to seeing you later," he declared. It wasn't a request, and by the way that her iridescent gaze slammed back to his, she recognized that.

"For your sake, Mr. Adorite, I hope you're comfortable with disappointment then." With that, she turned and took two steps in the opposite direction, glancing back at him over her bare shoulder as she said, "Because as far as you and I are concerned, that's all I have to offer you."

Another challenge. He liked that about her, as well.

Max watched her go, admiring the sleek lines of her curvy, petite body, the smooth, golden skin of her back, which was completely bare in that halter dress, the generous flare of her hips…

He wondered if she was as soft to the touch as she appeared.

Yes, Courtney Kogan was a decadent temptation, one he hadn't allowed himself in quite some time.

And Max found himself craving more of her.

He kept his eye on her as she slipped into the crowd, mingling with some of his high-profile guests, including a state senator, a couple of local judges, an overabundance of his own organization, along with, yes, a few of his enemies. What was the saying? Keep your friends close but your enemies closer? That was one he took to heart.

Max glanced to his side when a large body appeared in his peripheral vision.

"Anything you need, sir?" Leyton asked, his keen eyes scanning the room as he stood beside Max.

"I've got some preliminary information, but I want you to find out what you can on her," Max instructed, nodding his head toward Courtney. "Everything you can."

"Yes, sir."

With Leyton's help and some more personal inquiry, by the end of the night, Max fully intended to know more about Miss Kogan.

A lot more.

□»«□»«□»«□

"Max! Oh, God! We... Max! We can't do this." Courtney knew her denial sounded lame, especially since she was breathless, moaning, and clutching Max to her, giving in to the wonder that was his mouth.

The man could kiss, she'd give him that.

Although this... She wasn't sure this was classified as a mere kiss.

No, the way he crushed her between his impressive body and the wall, his rock-hard cock pressed against her belly, his muscular thigh grinding against her sex, his strong hands cupping her head, his determined tongue delving into her mouth…

No. This wasn't a kiss.

This was a claiming.

And Courtney was giving in to the intoxicating pleasure although she knew she shouldn't. Hell, she still wasn't entirely sure how she'd gotten to this point, making out in an empty hallway, plastered to the wall by the glorious weight of this man.

For the better part of the night, she'd kept a safe distance between herself and Maximillian Andrew Adorite and thought—apparently in error—that she'd managed to stay off his radar. But then, after she'd mingled a couple of hours with the people closest to him and had a few glasses of champagne, he'd asked her to dance. Which, now that she thought about it, had led to this heated make-out session.

Oh, God!

"*Max,*" *she said breathlessly.* "*Please, I…*" What the hell was she trying to say?

Another moan escaped her.

If he kept doing that, she was going to come.

"*You want this as much as I do,*" *he groaned as his mouth trailed down her neck, the smooth skin of his clean-shaven jaw brushing against her cheek, his warm lips leaving a path of fire in their wake. He smelled good, like musk and man and … sex.*

159

Sliding her fingers into the silky dark hair at the back of his head, Courtney pulled him closer, holding him to her, while his big, strong hand slid over her shoulder, drifted down her bare back, toward the curve of her waist and then farther, coming to rest briefly on her hip. He squeezed her gently before gliding his palm over her ass and down the back of her thigh.

His touch was exquisite. Powerful, determined. And she found herself defenseless against the onslaught of desire that sizzled in her veins, setting every nerve ending on fire.

When he lifted her thigh to his hip, bent his knees slightly, and adjusted their positions so that she was no longer riding his thigh, Courtney thought she would detonate. Now, she was...

"Max!" The erotic grind of his thick, rigid cock against her clit nearly sent her over the edge. When his mouth returned to hers, his teeth nipping her lower lip before sucking on it, the pleasure-pain had her hovering on the brink of orgasm.

Oh, God, yes!

Never once in her twenty-four years had she had a reaction to anyone like this. That all-encompassing need, the desperate, almost painful ache to be surrounded by him, filled by him. She'd always been daring and wild, but underneath that reckless exterior, Courtney's decisions were carefully thought out.

This wasn't what she'd consider careful.

Making out—in plain sight of anyone who cared to take a trip down this hallway—with Maximillian Adorite, the oldest child of Samuel David Adorite, the official crime boss of the Adorite family, otherwise known as the Southern Boy Mafia. More accurately, she was making out with the oldest son, the heir to the throne, so to speak, of one of the wealthiest—not to mention deadliest—families in Texas.

Technically, Max's status had just been upgraded, and Courtney was now lip-locked with the recently instated underboss, something she couldn't lose sight of, no matter how good his mouth was.

Max.

The same man who was making his power known tonight to those who would be working with him going forward—not to mention to her, although this particular expression of power was an entirely different type of conversation.

The changing of the guard, as her father had referred to it, was the reason for this party, the sole explanation as to why she was there to gather information for the client who'd hired Sniper 1 Security, her family's business.

Oh, God! Why me?

"*Max.*" *Courtney could hardly speak, the pleasure robbing her of her common sense, making her want things she was usually smart enough to resist.*

"Stay with me tonight," Max insisted, his head lifting, his sparkling honey-gold eyes meeting hers as he released her leg and brought his large palms up to cup her face. His thumbs gently skimmed her cheeks as he held her head firmly between his hands once again.

He was so big, so broad, so … there.

At six foot, Max's presence was felt as well as seen, the power that radiated from him palpable. He made her feel feminine, almost delicate, and definitely smaller than her five foot four inches. So much smaller.

Aside from how hot he made her, there was so much about the man she should fear, including who and what he was, but she couldn't seem to keep her hands off him.

Trying to fight the desire, to listen to the warning bells clanging in her head, Courtney shook her head, swallowed hard.

"I can see it in your eyes, Courtney." The rough, deep tenor of his voice resonated along her nerve endings, making her ache for him. "You want to stay with me. You want to feel me inside you, to feel me against you, skin to skin."

Again, she shook her head. It was a lie, but one she was sticking to. She *did* want him, did want to feel him inside her, to sweep her fingers along his naked flesh and touch the rock-hard body beneath the expensive tuxedo while he fucked her into a mind-numbing euphoria.

But that was stupid.

That *was* reckless.

Max's thumbs pressed against her chin, his palms cupping her jaw, fingers splayed along the back of her neck, as he tilted her head so that she had no choice but to look up into his eyes. Her body succumbed to the ecstasy of his touch as he pressed against her, his hard, muscular thigh once again sliding between her legs, grinding against her pussy, waves of pleasure crashing inside her, intensifying until she could hardly breathe for wanting this man.

Thankfully, she had an ounce of common sense left.

"No." She made sure there was no mistaking her adamant denial that time.

And just as she had hoped he would, Max released her, slowly stepping back, but his piercing gaze still pinned her in place.

"I'll never force you, Courtney. But I will have you. Make no mistake, I will have you in my bed, where you'll be beggin' me to make you come. It will happen."

Courtney swallowed hard. She hated him. Hated what he did to her. Hated how much she wanted him, despite knowing better. Hated that, when it came to him, her body seemed to be making all the decisions.

But more importantly, Courtney hated him for the man he was.

Despite the lavish exterior—mocha-brown hair and glowing gold eyes, a sexy body, and exquisite mouth—Courtney knew exactly who this man was beneath it all. No matter how attractive or polished he looked on the outside, Max wasn't the man he appeared to be.

He was evil. Pure and simple. A killer.

And her mission was to get information on him and his family, the transfer of power, the businesses that they ran … not to get into his bed. Yet here she was, battling with her conscience, weighing the difference between right and wrong, good and bad.

Righting her dress and sliding her hand over her hair in an effort to tame it, Courtney stood straight and squared her shoulders. "Tell yourself whatever you have to in order to sleep at night, Mr. Adorite. But make no mistake," she said, throwing his words back at him, "it will never happen."

To her surprise, Max didn't argue, but the smirk that flirted with the corners of his mouth said more than words.

"Good night, Mr. Adorite," she told him, turning and walking away without looking back.

As she headed back to the ballroom, where the party was still going strong, Courtney felt his eyes penetrating her, the same as they'd done for most of the night. She inhaled deeply, trying to regain her composure.

That man…

Damn it.

Fighting the urge to turn back and run into his arms, Courtney rounded the corner, grateful that no one was there to see her loss of equanimity as she leaned her back against the wall, her breaths coming in shallow and rushed. Her body was on fire, her insides melting from the pleasure his touch had promised.

How had she gotten herself into this position? How in the hell had she allowed herself to be seduced by Maximillian Adorite? A freaking gangster.

Get a hold of yourself.

Taking a long, deep breath, then exhaling slowly, she stood straight once more, refusing to let him win this round.

Walking away from Max was the smart choice. Her only choice. And as her breathing returned to normal, she made up her mind to do just that.

Not that she thought Max was giving up. He was the type of man who got exactly what he wanted. And she understood that she presented a challenge to him. One that he would likely conquer eventually, but Courtney knew she had to walk away. And stay away.

Easier said than done.

Exhaling deeply, Courtney ignored the unnerving feeling that slammed into her … the one that told her, without a doubt, she was on a collision course that she couldn't repave, one that would end, based on what she'd just experienced tonight, either beautiful or brutal.

Then again, based on what she knew of the man, she was more inclined to believe it'd be beautifully brutal.

And part of her was anxious to find out.

The reckless part.

By Nicole Edwards

The Alluring Indulgence Series
Kaleb
Zane
Travis
Holidays with the Walker Brothers
Ethan
Braydon
Sawyer
Brendon

The Austin Arrows Series
Rush
Kaufman

The Bad Boys of Sports Series
Bad Reputation
Bad Business

The Caine Cousins Series
Hard to Hold
Hard to Handle

The Club Destiny Series
Conviction
Temptation
Addicted
Seduction
Infatuation
Captivated
Devotion
Perception
Entrusted
Adored
Distraction

The Coyote Ridge Series
Curtis
Jared

The Dead Heat Ranch Series
Boots Optional
Betting on Grace
Overnight Love

By Nicole Edwards (cont.)

The Devil's Bend Series

Chasing Dreams
Vanishing Dreams

The Devil's Playground Series

Without Regret
Without Restraint

The Office Intrigue Series

Office Intrigue
Intrigued Out of the Office
Their Rebellious Submissive

The Pier 70 Series

Reckless
Fearless
Speechless
Harmless

The Sniper 1 Security Series

Wait for Morning
Never Say Never
Tomorrow's Too Late

The Southern Boy Mafia Series

Beautifully Brutal
Beautifully Loyal

Standalone Novels

A Million Tiny Pieces
Inked on Paper

Writing as Timberlyn Scott

Unhinged
Unraveling
Chaos

Naughty Holiday Editions

2015
2016

Made in the USA
Monee, IL
10 June 2020